Shotgun Ridge, Montana, was founded in the 1800s by Addie Malone, a woman brave enough to take on five thieves and strong enough to tame the land around her. Now the town needed more women like Addie to rustle up its bachelors, make roots and keep Shotgun Ridge thriving. Four matchmaking old men were determined to help nature take its course, and this time they've decided Stony Stratton, town loner, would be the next bachelor to tie the knot.

***

"Marry me."

Eden stared at Stony, heard the whinny of horses outside. "Excuse me?"

"I understand what you need," he said quietly.

"Marriage?" Eden's head was suddenly spinning.

"With stipulations. We'll give the marriage six months. If you're not pregnant by then, we'll call it quits. Before you answer, though, there's something I need to do."

"Of course—"

His gaze dropped to her mouth and her words dried up.

Oh, she thought. He meant he needed to do something right this very minute....

Dear Reader,

Come join us for another dream-fulfilling month of Harlequin American Romance! We're proud to have this chance to bring you our four special new stories.

In her brand-new miniseries, beloved author Cathy Gillen Thacker will sweep you away to Laramie, Texas, hometown of matchmaking madness for THE LOCKHARTS OF TEXAS. Trouble brews when arch rivals Beau and Dani discover a marriage license—with their names on it! Don't miss *The Bride Said, "I Did?"*!

What better way to turn a bachelor's mind to matrimony than sending him a woman who desperately needs to have a baby? Mindy Neff continues her legendary BACHELORS OF SHOTGUN RIDGE miniseries this month with *The Horseman's Convenient Wife*—watch Eden and Stony discover that love is anything but convenient!

Imagine waking up to see your own wedding announcement in the paper—to someone you hardly know! Melinda has some explaining to do to Ben in Mollie Molay's *The Groom Came C.O.D.*, the first book in our HAPPILY WEDDED AFTER promotion. And in Kara Lennox's *Virgin Promise*, a bad boy is shocked to discover he's seduced a virgin. Will promising to court her from afar convince her he wants more than one night of passion?

Find out this month, only from Harlequin American Romance!

Best wishes,
Melissa Jeglinski
Associate Senior Editor

The Horseman's Convenient Wife

MINDY NEFF

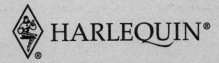

HARLEQUIN®

TORONTO • NEW YORK • LONDON
AMSTERDAM • PARIS • SYDNEY • HAMBURG
STOCKHOLM • ATHENS • TOKYO • MILAN • MADRID
PRAGUE • WARSAW • BUDAPEST • AUCKLAND

To Patricia Thayer Wright,
A wonderful writer and friend. Fate sat us next to each
other at that very first conference. Friendship took it
from there. Thanks, Pat, for the endless hours of plotting,
the gab and the whine sessions, and for just being there.
And special thanks to Anita Lynn Gunnufson for your
fabulous medical expertise!

ISBN 0-373-16838-1

THE HORSEMAN'S CONVENIENT WIFE

Copyright © 2000 by Melinda Neff.

Visit us at www.eHarlequin.com

Printed in U.S.A.

ABOUT THE AUTHOR

Originally from Louisiana, Mindy Neff settled in Southern California, where she married a really romantic guy and raised five great kids. Family, friends, writing and reading are her passions. When not writing, Mindy's ideal getaway is a good book, hot sunshine and a chair at the river's edge with water lapping at her toes.

Mindy loves to hear from readers and can be reached at P.O. Box 2704-262, Huntington Beach, CA 92647.

Books by Mindy Neff

HARLEQUIN AMERICAN ROMANCE

~Tall, Dark & Irresistible
*Bachelors of Shotgun Ridge

Don't miss any of our special offers. Write to us at the following address for information on our newest releases.

Harlequin Reader Service
U.S.: 3010 Walden Ave., P.O. Box 1325, Buffalo, NY 14269
Canadian: P.O. Box 609, Fort Erie, Ont. L2A 5X3

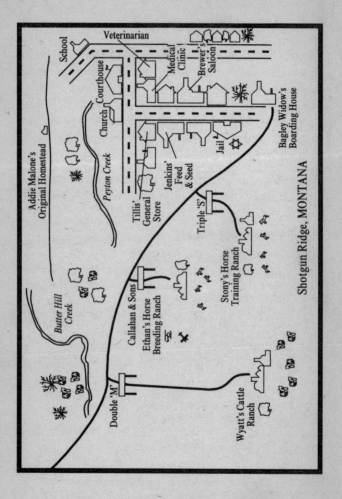

Shotgun Ridge, MONTANA

Prologue

Ah, things are progressing nicely with these stubborn cowboys—even if I do say so myself.

Ozzie Peyton gave a jaunty wink to the portrait over the fireplace and was fairly certain his sweet Vanessa winked back. The love of his life, she'd gone to the hereafter just last year, and it was a balm to his soul that she still spoke to him now and again to keep him on track and save the days and long nights from being so lonely. She didn't approve of every little decision he made, but she was such a good woman about it.

She'd always been that way, and it was a crying shame they'd never been blessed with children of their own. Vanessa, a schoolteacher all her life, would have been the best of mothers.

Realizing he was digressing, Ozzie turned his attention back to his journal writing.

In our wildest dreams, Lloyd, Henry, Vern and me never dreamed things would turn out so good. We're still takin' our time so as not to make any rash or wrong moves. And so far so good. But as my Vanessa has told me, we can't be takin' over the good Lord's job too much—even though I pointed out that we was just helpin' since He is likely a busy man and could use the extra hand or two to lay the groundwork.

But here I go again, getting off the subject. That's been happenin' a lot lately. Maybe I ought to try me some of them new herbs that're supposed to boost the brainpower.

Anyway, Wyatt and Hannah Malone are happy as all get-out and make the best family picture with that cute little boy of Hannah's, Ian, and Hannah with her tummy all round with child. Not Wyatt's seed, but his child nonetheless. That boy's power to love just plum amazes me. And it especially touches my heart on account of Vanessa and me not having the pitter-patter of little feet in our own home.

And Ethan and Dora Callahan. There was a long shot if I ever thought of one. A preacher's daughter and a playboy cowboy, whose carousing days actually did come back to bite him in the keister. But that baby girl, Katie...I tell you, she's a cutie. And Dora, feisty little thing, just the match for Ethan. The boy never knew what hit him. 'Course when I heard about the puppy poop in the boots and the kitten hair in the hat, me and Vern and Henry and Lloyd had a bit of a pause. After all, a cowboy's boots and hat are sacred. But ya just can't get all het up over Dora and her taking in every stray animal and making those cute drawings of them that she sells to greetin' card companies and the like.

So, now we've had us a good success with advertising for women in the magazines, and that bachelor auction that gave us all a new set of wiry gray hairs. But all turned out for the best. And we got plenty of women who've come to town and are thinking of stayin'.

Now that's all well and good, but ya just never know what'll happen if somebody drops the ball. That's what me, Vern, Lloyd and Henry were just talkin' about the other day.

And that's how come we decided to give Stony Stratton a bit of a nudge. A nicer fellow you'd never meet. But he don't know the value of his qualities. And that sweet little girl of his, just cryin' out for a mama—not that Stony's not doing a mighty fine job all on his own. But still, there's work to be done here.

So when Lottie told us about Eden Williams's problems, the boys and me couldn't help but have our hearts ripping open and bleeding a bit at the shame of it all. Especially seeing as how our purpose is to show the men of Shotgun Ridge the merits of marriage and procreating, just like the Good Lord intended.

Vanessa wasn't happy about that little lie we done told, but she's a forgiving woman, and in the end I think she secretly believes we done right—she's just got to keep up her fussin' at me for appearance sake, and I sure do love her for that.

Besides, it was only one of them white lies…well, all right, it was dingy white with a bit of gray around the edges, but still, we got a responsibility to uphold, to our town and to our future.

We've laid the path. Now we just gotta hope old Stony Stratton will walk on down it. Especially when he hears exactly what Eden Williams wants—no, what she *needs* from him....

Chapter One

Stony Stratton leaned against the porch rail and watched the racy convertible spit dust beneath its tires as it barreled toward the ranch. In the paddocks, million-dollar Thoroughbreds lifted elegant heads, nostrils flaring, tracking the progress of the sporty car as it whizzed past stables, the round training pens and storage barns, then wheeled up the circular driveway toward the house.

Another interruption in a list of many, these past three days, Stony thought. Normally he was a pretty easygoing guy. But his life had suddenly turned upside down, and his frustration level was creeping up.

He still couldn't believe his housekeeper had taken off on him the way she had. Lottie Driscol and her husband, Ray, had been with him for fifteen years. They'd cried with him when his grandmother had died and bolstered him during the two years of his disastrous marriage.

The woman was as sturdy as they came, had faced rattlers in the yard, blizzards, a skunk rooting in the kitchen pantry, bloody cowboys who'd tangled with an ornery stallion, and the death of a child, yet an accidental fire set to the kitchen curtains several days ago had sent her into a dither.

In a fit of dramatics, his steady, practical housekeeper had packed her bags, claiming she needed a vacation, and had abandoned him, taking her husband—who was their all-around handyman—with her. It was the damnedest thing. So out of character.

If he wasn't so level-headed, he might think the townsfolk had somehow roped Lottie into their crazy conspiracy to marry off the bachelors of Shotgun Ridge. But that scenario didn't seem to fit, and he'd already concluded he was fairly safe on that score.

Stony knew what he saw in the mirror every morning, and he didn't kid himself. He didn't have the looks his friends and neighbors, Wyatt Malone and Ethan Callahan, had. He was a big hulk, who communicated better with animals than he did with people.

And according to his ex-wife, there wasn't much to recommend him as husband material. He caught himself reaching for his face but checked the action, feeling his gut tighten in a way it hadn't in a long time.

He had no idea why he was thinking about the scheming geezers, other than the fact that he knew just about every vehicle in this part of Montana, and that fire-engine-red Mustang wasn't one he recognized. Nor was the woman driving it.

"Who's that, Daddy?"

With his gaze on the woman now alighting from the car, Stony held out his hand for his five-year-old daughter, Nicole.

"Let's go find out," he said quietly. Stony rarely

spoke above a strong murmur. He was a man who watched, listened.

He squinted against the sun and felt the scar at the side of his eye crinkle and fold in on itself. With Nikki's hand swallowed in his huge palm, he tugged his white Stetson lower on his brow and gave Nikki's dog a gentle command to stay.

The woman grabbed a guitar case from the back seat, turned in a circle to take in her surroundings, then smiled and moved forward, her right hand extended.

"Hi. I'm Eden Williams. My aunt Lottie told me you were looking for a housekeeper."

Her *aunt* Lottie? Stony tipped his head in a nod and accepted her handshake. My God she was beautiful. No way would she do as a live-in housekeeper-nanny. Beauty and the beast didn't cohabit well.

"And this must be Nicole," she said, dropping to one knee in front of the little girl while Stony was still trying to corral his heart.

"Yep," Nikki confirmed. "You talk funny."

"Nikki," Stony admonished gently.

"Well, she does."

Eden laughed. "It's my Texas accent. So, what do you think? Is it a good kind of funny or a weird kind?"

Nikki considered for a minute. "Good kind. Did you know Lottie catched the curtains on fire?"

"Mmm, that's sort of why I'm here."

"Are *you* gonna catch the curtains on fire?"

"No, silly." Her laughter was soft and genuine. "I'm here to take care of you and your daddy."

Ah, hell. He wished she hadn't said anything in front of Nikki. Now he was going to have to come up with a good excuse for not hiring her and explain it to both the woman *and* his daughter.

"What's in there?" Nikki pointed to the gleaming rosewood case at Eden's feet.

"My guitar. I like to think I can carry a tune, and a little background music disguises the rough spots. Do you like to sing?"

Nikki nodded. "My uncle Ethan—well, he's not *really* my uncle, but sort of, you know?"

Eden nodded and Stony realized he had yet to speak to her or take his gaze from her. Her auburn hair was long and straight, curling slightly at the ends, held back off her face by glittering butterfly clips. With her flared jeans and snug top, she looked a bit like a sixties flower child.

"Anyway," Nikki continued, "Uncle Ethan teached me numbers with the bottles of beer, but Daddy didn't think it was 'propriate, so we had to do it with milk. Want me to sing it for you?"

Before Stony could object, Eden nodded and Nikki belted out the first notes.

"'One bottle of milk on the wall, one bottle of milk, put one up and go back to the truck, and there's two bottles of milk on the wall.'" She went through several more verses, holding out another finger each time to keep track of which number she was on.

"That's wonderful," Eden said. "And ingenious to go forward rather than backward." She stood and swayed slightly.

Stony immediately reached out to steady her. "Careful." It was his natural instinct to protect—an ingrained trait.

"Thanks." Her smile knocked him straight in the

solar plexus, and he told himself to get a grip. She didn't need him to take care of her. The woman was looking for a job. That's all she would want from him.

"You have a beautiful place here." She looked out at the ranch, but Stony kept his gaze on her. "Aunt Lottie said you're a horse whisperer?"

"Trainer," he corrected.

"And in mighty tall cotton by the look of the place."

Tall…? Oh. *Successful.* He shrugged, not one to boast.

She gave him another soft smile, this one obviously for his modesty, and he noted twin dimples in her pale cheeks. Her coloring was different from that of skin simply kept out of the sun. The darkness beneath her eyes made him wonder if she'd been ill. And he had no business wondering about Eden Williams's health.

"Being family and all, I'm surprised you've never been out to visit your aunt and uncle."

"Aunt Lottie's a lot like your Nikki's Ethan, I suspect. She was my mom's best friend and lived close by throughout my growing up years. Not related by blood, but loved nonetheless."

"Like me and Daddy," Nikki said.

Eden looked from the little girl to him. Stony wasn't in the mood to go into his background with a virtual stranger. She'd more than likely not be staying.

He cupped Nikki's shoulder. "Nik, why don't you take Rosie in and feed her."

"Oh." Nikki glanced at the dog, then her brows suddenly winged up. She lifted one of the black setter's ears, whispered into it, then dropped it back in place and straightened. "Okay. Rosie said she's hungry. Come in and see my room, Eden." Full of energy, she took off like a shot, bounding up the porch steps with the dog on her heels.

"She's a doll baby," Eden said.

"Yes." And up to something, he thought with an inward sigh. He'd seen it in the sparkle of her eye. "How long have you been in town?"

"Not long. I came when Aunt Lottie called."

He saw her glance away. It was a subtle shift, but he was trained to notice nuances. Being raised by a deaf grandmother who'd communicated with gestures and expressions made him sensitive to the actions of others. It's what gave him an edge with the animals and made him who he was.

He wondered what Eden Williams was hiding.

"Lottie called you?"

"Mmm. She really hated to leave you in the lurch."

Stony nearly snorted, but merely frowned instead. He didn't recall Lottie seeming all that concerned when she'd been pressing her hand to her bosom and imitating a drama queen.

"So…you just came out? No questions asked? You don't have another job waiting for you back in Texas?" Lottie had left three days ago. Eden would have had to react immediately, dropping everything to get to Montana to take her aunt's place.

"Actually, I did ask a few questions," she said softly, her green eyes focusing on him with what appeared to be hope and trust. She didn't elaborate on what those questions had been, and Stony found himself suddenly and inexplicably curious.

"As for my job," she continued, "I'm partners in a catering business. But I needed time off."

Obviously that runs in the family, he thought. "Why?"

There it was again. That subtle skittering of her eyes, a blink.

"I just needed time for me. I've been so caught up in work I hadn't realized I'd neglected some personal things that are important to me. Aunt Lottie suggested I come to Shotgun Ridge, that it would be a nice change of pace."

"For how long?"

She shrugged. "For a while, at least. There's no telling how long it'll take Aunt Lottie to get over her stress…." She laughed and touched his arm. "I understand that look. And believe me, I was as surprised as you when she told me the story about the curtains and the need for time off because of it. In any case, you'll be getting a great deal. I love kids and I'm an excellent cook."

He shouldn't even be considering this. He'd had someone more matronly in mind for the job. But so far none of the older women in town had responded to his plea for help—and he hadn't dared ask any of the single women new to town that Ozzie and his friends had rounded up with their crazy marriage campaign.

He wasn't stepping into that trap.

"Where are you staying?"

She frowned. "I thought…well, um, here, of course."

He didn't see that there was any "of course" about it. He only needed help during the day. The evenings he could handle himself.

Aside from the fact that having a beautiful woman live with him would drive him to distraction, Nikki was young and impressionable. Clearly, Eden Williams was a woman who would be easy to fall in love with. And Nikki fell in love easily. To form an attachment, only to have Eden leave, would be hard on her.

And Stony didn't kid himself that she would stay. Beautiful women didn't. Unless they were paid handsomely or were offered something valuable in return. And even then there were no guarantees.

He turned his head slightly to the right, a subconscious gesture to shield the flawed part of his face.

"I hadn't planned to hire someone full-time or permanent." Especially a beautiful young woman with pale skin and green eyes and a body that made him yearn. "I'd heard the Widows Bagley were renting out rooms in town."

"Oh, no. I need to stay here....I mean, it'll be much more convenient. Lottie and Ray had a room, didn't they?" There was desperation in her tone and a slight tremble in her fingers as she clasped them together in front of her.

His protective instincts reared again, and he tried like crazy to ignore them. "They had a room. But it's just Nikki and me in the house."

"And isn't that why you need me?"

He had a sinking feeling he could come to need her too much. And in a much different way. "I meant that it might not look proper—you being so young and all."

Her laughter startled a magpie off the fence post and held Stony spellbound for several seconds. The drum of hooves as one of the handlers put a horse through its paces faded into the background.

"I'm thirty-four, Stony. Hardly a young maiden in need of a chaperone."

Those killer dimples might well get the better of him. As it was, his judgment was skewed. That was the only explanation he could come up with when he found himself looking toward her flashy convertible, asking her if she had luggage, inviting her inside. Sometimes he wondered if he was a throwback to another era. He didn't think or operate in the free-and-easy, casual way that most of his friends did.

Eden followed Stony around the back of the house and in through the kitchen door. Apparently, he was used to entering this way—not suggesting she use the back door like the help. She smiled to herself and imagined he'd be horrified if she made mention of it, even in jest.

Lottie had told her quite a bit about Stony Stratton. A giant, Gentle Ben type, she'd said, who speaks softly to women and children, leaving melted hearts in his wake—and he never even recognized it. A tough, six-foot-five cowboy with a fierce frown and a heart as big as Texas.

And Eden was counting on that big heart. She was on a mission, and the clock was ticking.

Stony Stratton was her hope.

She felt the familiar lethargy pull at her and pressed a hand to her stomach. *Not yet,* she prayed. *Please, just give me a week to settle in.*

Her weariness abated somewhat when she got a look at the kitchen. A chef would be in hog heaven for sure. It had to be twenty by twenty in size, with a work station in the center, cabinets galore painted glossy white with crystal knobs, a restaurant-grade stove and sparkling, rich granite countertops. The room was clean and straight except for a step stool pushed up against the refrigerator and an open pantry door.

"Oh, my." Her reverent tone drew Stony's gaze. His eyes softened and smiled, but his lips didn't follow. That was okay. Lottie had warned Eden about his solemn countenance, but hadn't gone into detail about what might have made him that way.

"Lottie supervised a remodeling project a few years back."

"I know. Since I cook for a living, she consulted me on a couple of things. I feel as though I'm getting reacquainted with an old friend." She ran a hand over the mirror-smooth granite and smiled softly when a little girl's delighted giggle rang out. Following the sound, she peeked behind the open pantry door where Nikki was hiding.

Eden's smile turned to a grin. Nikki was giving the black Irish setter a lick of her frozen juice bar.

She glanced at Stony. "Guess we know what Nikki and Rosie were whispering about outside." She didn't imagine this was what he'd had in mind when he'd asked his daughter to feed the dog.

"Look, Daddy! She likes it."

"So I see," Stony said, his tone easy and even. "Remember that she doesn't do well with too many sweets." For Eden's benefit he added, "There was an incident a while back with the contents of the sugar bowl at Nikki's pretend tea party. It got messy."

"Yeah, Rosie barfed, and Lottie wouldn't clean it up."

"I'm sure Rosie didn't mean to barf," Eden said, and Nikki went into a gale of giggles, pulling her hand back to have a lick of sticky red ice that dripped down her little arm.

The sound of a happy child wrapped itself around Eden's heart and squeezed. Unbidden, a lump formed in her throat.

She turned to Stony, startled to find him watching her. Quietly. Easily. Steadily. A funny tickle shivered through her stomach, and she wasn't sure if it was nerves or attraction. A little of both, she suspected.

He was overwhelmingly big, yet she didn't feel threatened. Excited, yes, and scared, but of her own feelings, not of him.

Eden broke eye contact first. Clearing her throat, she tugged at her top. "Well…"

He nodded as though acknowledging her nervousness. "I'll show you Lottie and Ray's room." Picking up her suitcase, he exited the kitchen by way of the service porch. A glance over his shoulder at Rosie had the dog's ears drooping and with a final longing look at the ice pop, she lay down and rested her muzzle on her front paws.

Eden was impressed. Watching the dog instead of where she was going, she slammed into Stony's back when he stopped at the threshold of a suite of rooms off the kitchen.

"Steady," he said.

"Yes…well." She couldn't recall ever being so tongue-tied around a man. "Were you and Rosie communicating telepathically?"

"No need. She knows what's allowed and what's not."

He set her suitcase on the bed, then turned around, those amber eyes focusing on hers with an intensity she was coming to expect. It was as though he saw inside her, and that unnerved her even more.

She wasn't ready for him to see her flaws—or her quiet desperation.

"You're tired." He raised his hand, as though he intended to touch her face, then let it drop as he stepped back. "Rest awhile, settle in, then we'll talk about the terms of employment—salary and such."

With an economy of moves, he left the room, his boot heels barely making a sound against the hardwood floor, which was surprising given his size.

When he was gone, she lowered herself to the bed, momentarily giving in to the lack of energy, feeling a twinge of the cramping that had become all too familiar.

She would rest for just a few minutes, she promised herself as she closed her eyes, holding the edge of the bedspread in her hands.

Stony Stratton was everything Aunt Lottie had said he'd be...and more.

He didn't have the smooth, pretty-boy looks of a male print model, but he had something even better. He had presence, a masculinity that radiated from him in sensual waves. A quiet reverence and inner spirit that spoke loud and clear, even when he didn't.

He was a man who would care. And care deeply.

She vowed to be very careful with his heart.

The urge to rush was almost overwhelming. But she cautioned herself to slow down, give him a chance to warm up to her before she told him her real reason for coming.

The reason Aunt Lottie had invented that cockamamy story so she could leave.

Chapter Two

Instead of a quick nap, Eden slept through the night. When she woke, she was still dressed in her jeans and snug blue T-shirt, but her shoes were off and she was all the way in the bed, covered with a crisp cotton sheet and a soft chenille bedspread.

Her heart bumped against her rib cage as a wave of confusion and embarrassment washed through her. She remembered sitting on the bed, lying back, her feet still on the floor. And now…

"Oh, my gosh." She leaped up, felt light-headed and took a moment to clear the flash of white dots dancing in her vision like Fourth of July sparklers. This was *not* the way to start a new job.

Horrified, forming apologies in her mind, she quickly changed and brushed her teeth, then poured out a handful of vitamins and iron tablets, made her way to the kitchen and downed them with a glass of orange juice. Grabbing a piece of raisin bread out of the bread box, she went out the kitchen door in search of Stony.

She saw him leaning against the paddock fence and she nearly stumbled. He was a very, *very* fine specimen of the male form.

As she approached, he held out a hand, nearly brushing her abdomen, yet he never took his eyes off the beautiful stallion in the fenced pen. She understood his gesture and stopped beside him, stood quietly and waited.

And while he kept his gaze focused on the magnificent animal, Eden was riveted by the magnificent man. A pair of leather chaps hugged his legs, buckled low on his hips and tied at the tops of his thighs. An oversize silver buckle decorated his belt, drawing her attention to the area of his dark jeans framed by the sexy protective gear.

She told herself she shouldn't dwell there, yet her eyes seemed to have a will of their own for several long breathtaking seconds. With great effort she dragged her gaze upward to the white shirt that stretched across his wide shoulders. He wore a brown bandanna tied around his neck and the ever-present white hat that added a good six inches to his already-impressive six-and-a-half-foot frame.

Eden considered herself above average in height, but next to Stony she felt positively puny.

And very feminine.

"See the ears?" He spoke softly, his voice deep and even. "One's forward and the other's back. He's interested in us, but he's wary, too."

"How do you know?" Eden's voice, too, was quiet—a little like whispering in the library.

"Horses communicate. If you watch them, listen, pay attention, they'll talk to you. See there?" He gave a nod that barely tipped his hat, but he didn't point or make any sudden moves other than to turn slightly toward her. "His ears are flicking back and forth, and his nostrils are blowing. He's asking us what's going on. Why is he here, what do we want, what's the drill?''

She felt the warmth radiating from Stony's chest and nearly became sidetracked. He'd bent subtly toward her—an unconscious habit of a big man—so that his lips were close to her head, his breath stirring the hair at her temple.

"He's a beautiful horse," she said. "Not one of yours, though?"

"Owner had him trucked in last night. Seems he's developed a nasty habit of biting, and he spooks at the slightest sound.''

"And they're hiring you to cure him of it?"

He tipped his head, shifted, and their shoulders brushed. She drew in a breath and felt his gaze on her now. She looked up into whiskey-colored eyes that watched rather than stared.

The size of him, his quiet assurance, had a way of wrapping a woman in a cocoon of safety.

Her gaze shifted to the scar that sliced through his brow and along the outer rim of his eye, and she felt him withdraw. He was self-conscious, she realized. Yet why would he be? Did he think it diminished him in some way? She wondered if he'd been injured by a horse, but knew enough not to press. They were still at the ''getting used to each other'' stage.

And as much as she would like to rush the process, her goal was too important to risk. She had to have patience.

"What's his name?"

He glanced back at the horse. "Fox-Trot Dandy."

"Dandy? Are you kidding? He looks much too

macho to be called a dandy. Who's the idiot who thought that up?''

He looked down at her, his eyes amused. ''The idiot who owns Fox-Trot's sire, I imagine. Tango Dandy's a Triple Crown winner worth several million.''

''Well then, I guess the name hasn't dented their egos any.'' She flicked her hair behind her ear, gaining a whole new perspective and respect for the sleek, beautiful animals—and for Stony Stratton. There was an absolute fortune on this ranch. ''So, if this big guy's gotten so jumpy, why aren't our voices and movements spooking him?''

''He knows we're here. We haven't startled him, just made him curious.''

''You can tell that by just looking at him?''

''Watching,'' he corrected. ''See there. He's annoyed that we're talking and not keeping him the center of attention.''

''Mmm. Typical male.'' Her heart leaped when he gave her another of those indulgent looks where his eyes softened. Too bad his mouth didn't curve to match. If he'd cut loose and smile, the man would be positively lethal to the opposite sex. ''So what can you tell about this one?''

He turned back to the stallion. ''He's cocky and proud, but he doesn't strike me as a crazy horse. He's got an intelligent head, alert eyes. I'd say he's looking for somebody he can trust, a handler who'll let him offer cooperation rather than insist on it.''

She frowned. ''Are you saying someone's been cruel to him?''

''No. But something's got him upset recently, and if we don't get to the bottom of it, someone will likely end up getting hurt.'' He spread the fingers on his hand and took a step forward.

The stallion's head jerked up, and he took off to the far corner of the pen. With a scream of rage, his ears pinned and he charged forward, heading straight for them, every vibrating, quivering muscle in his sleek, powerful body radiating anger and aggression.

Eden gave a squeak of fright, grabbed a handful of Stony's shirt and hid behind him, sure that they were both about to be trod into the dirt.

Stony stood perfectly still.

Snorting, hooves kicking up a cloud of dust, the stallion skidded to a halt mere feet from the wooden fence in front of them.

Eden had no doubt that the powerful horse could have burst right through the fence if he'd chosen to. She peeked out from behind Stony's broad shoulder, saw the horse toss his head, up and down, mane flying in the breeze.

Frightened, yet awed, she watched as the stallion arrogantly looked down his nose, fixing his eyes on Stony, each taking the other's measure. Danger sizzled in the air, as well as power.

''I'm not backing down, buddy.'' Stony's words were delivered in a quiet, soothing tone, like a parent assuring a child who feared abandonment.

Eden thought he surely ought to reconsider, but kept the opinion to herself.

For several long seconds an eerie sort of communication seemed to take place between man and animal.

Then the stallion jerked his head higher, one ear trained on Stony, and began to prance, all the while watching them. His movements were deliberate, aggressive, radiating pride and an arrogant taunt.

Shivering, Eden unfisted the wad of shirt she'd been clutching and cautiously came out from behind the protection of Stony's back. She didn't even pretend to be embarrassed or coy over her cowardice. That horse had scared the daylights out of her, and she didn't have a qualm in the world about admitting it.

"He's daring you to cross into his territory, isn't he?"

Stony nodded. "He doesn't know me or trust me. I expected as much. We'll let him be for a while. I'll come back and work with him a little later."

"You're going to go in the pen with him?" There was no way to keep the horror out of her tone.

"That's usually what it takes."

"Are you crazy? He's bigger than you. Won't he bite you? Or trample you to death?"

His lips very nearly curved. "Hope not."

He was so nonchalant. "Fine, then. It's your funeral. I trust you have your insurance premiums paid up?"

He cocked a brow and dipped his head.

"You can be awfully stingy with your words," she muttered. "So how long have you been doing this sort of thing?"

"Since I was four."

"You hauled yourself up on snapping stallions when you were four years old?"

"I think I steered clear of the snapping ones until I was at least six."

She punched him playfully on the arm. "You're making fun of me."

He went still at that. Like a cloud passing over
the sun, momentary astonishment changed to absolute seriousness. "No. I don't make fun."

She'd hit a nerve without realizing it.

"Do you *have* fun?" she asked softly.

"With Nikki around, a person has fun whether
they want to or not."

"Speaking of Nikki, I'm sorry I fell asleep on you
last night and then overslept this morning."

"No problem. You looked as though you needed
the rest."

She remembered waking up between the covers,
knew he would have had to lift her to get her there,
knew that those large, gentle hands had taken off
her shoes, touched her skin. And she hadn't even
been awake to appreciate it.

"Nonetheless, I've never been so irresponsible on
the first day of a job in my life." Impulsively she
stood on tiptoe and brushed his cheek with a kiss.

The left one.

She wanted to press her lips to that scar on his
right side, but knew he would jerk and shy just like
that troubled stallion had.

"Thank you for taking care of me."

He shrugged, and for the first time since she'd
met him, he wouldn't hold her gaze. "My pleasure."

With a hand barely touching her back, he steered
her away from the paddock. Just that fleeting brush
of his fingertips, she realized, and he'd guided her
as surely as a dance instructor might guide a student.
His presence alone surrounded her, swept her along
beside him.

She shook her head, decided her blood count must

be dropping again and her brain was becoming mud-dled. Why else would she dwell on Stony Stratton's power of silent communication? If that's what it was.

Regardless, the quiet man beside her made her nerve endings hum.

She cleared her throat. "Where is Nikki?"

"Over in the stables with Demone."

Realizing they were heading in that direction, Eden watched the ranch activity going on all around them. Two horses were hooked to what looked like a giant pinwheel-shaped clothesline, walking con-tentedly in a circle, necks bowed and heads pointed downward as though they didn't have a care in the world. Another was in a round corral, a cowboy atop it. With its russet-colored coat gleaming in the July sun, the horse ran full-out, then suddenly skidded to a halt and spun around like a tightly wound ballerina on a music box.

"My gosh, that's so beautiful. How do y'all get them to do that?"

"Practice. Trust."

The way he looked at her when he said *trust* made her squirm. It was as though he knew she was hold-ing something back and asking her to trust him.

He didn't know how very much she *did* trust, how much she'd *had* to trust him in order to come here.

But she needed a little more time before she con-fided in him.

They stepped from the summer heat into the cool, shaded interior of the stables. The smell of animals, fresh hay and leather mingled together, creating its own special aroma. Stalls lined the wide concrete aisle, some standing open as men raked out soiled straw and forked in a clean layer.

She saw Nikki come out of the tack room, a plump, tiger-striped cat draped in her arms, Rosie trotting along beside her.

"Is that dog her bodyguard or her partner in crime?" she asked.

"A little of both," Stony said.

Eden stopped him with a hand on his arm. Nikki was so caught up in her conversation with the animals as she went into one of the open stalls, she hadn't yet seen them.

"How can you be around that little girl and not be smiling all the time?"

He frowned. "I *do* smile."

"When?"

"Now."

"You're kidding." With a laugh, she spied a dusty mirror hanging on the wall over a bench seat and turned him toward it.

She knew instantly that he didn't want to look. Muscles rigid with tension flexed beneath her palms.

Now it was her turn to frown.

He spun around, away from the mirror. "I know what my face looks like."

She couldn't believe it. This man actually believed he was unattractive. Who would have told him that? Made him believe it?

"Stony—"

"I need to get back to work."

She let out her breath in a sigh. It looked as though neither one of them was ready to extend any trust.

"Are there things I need to know? About the

job,'' she clarified when his narrowed eyes made it clear he thought she was trying to pry into his personal life. "Schedules and such.''

His shoulders relaxed some, and when he swallowed, his Adam's apple bobbed just above the brown bandanna tied at his throat. The movement nearly derailed Eden's thoughts.

He tugged his hat lower on his brow, the right side dipping slightly more than the left. Habit, she noted. Caused by a wound. A wound not on the surface, but etched on his heart.

"Nikki's pretty self-reliant. She's been on the ranch and around the animals since she was a baby. But she's got a keen curiosity, and although every man on the ranch watches out for her when she's around the horses and equipment, sometimes she slips out of our sight.''

Eden nodded. "So Aunt Lottie and Uncle Ray made it a point to accompany her when she went outdoors.''

"Not always. They had things to do, also. We just need a heads-up if she comes out by herself.''

"Got it. Notify the team on duty.'' She ignored his skeptical look. She adored kids and they adored her. She just didn't know how much freedom or supervision a five-year-old needed. That's why she was asking, for goodness sake.

"What about meals? So far I've counted six men out here working. Do you all eat together, and if so, are there set times?''

"I've got eight men working with me, but they take care of their own meals. Their housing is over in the west section—the gray building you passed on the way in yesterday.''

Eden actually felt relief. Although she'd catered parties of five hundred, her energy level lately wasn't what it used to be. The limitations annoyed her, made her heart ache if she dwelled on it.

"Okay. Anything else? Ballet lessons? Slumber parties scheduled?"

"No lessons. Hannah Malone sometimes brings her son, Ian, over to play, or Nikki goes over to their ranch. At five she doesn't have a real active social life," he said dryly.

Eden grinned. "Okay, no making fun. I'm trying to get the lay of the land here. I thought I had asked Aunt Lottie all the pertinent questions, but I realize I forgot some important points." Domestic ones. Housekeeping-nanny ones. She'd mainly asked her aunt about Stony Stratton.

Stony shrugged. "We live a pretty simple life out here. I'll take you into town if you like, introduce you around, show you where to get groceries and stuff."

"Oh, I can handle that myself. I stopped on my way in, anyway. Besides, I mingle well, never have had any trouble meeting folks."

"Right. I suppose your line of business is pretty social."

She grinned. "I could probably talk a magpie off a fence if I put my mind to it."

Stunned, delighted, she watched his lips curve ever so slightly. She held her breath, waited for him to go all the way, frustrated when he didn't.

It was a start, though. A wonderful start. This man needed to smile. To laugh. And she intended to see to it that he did.

Perhaps that could be her gift to him before she left.

Eden couldn't imagine what she would do if she couldn't laugh. Laughter kept away the doom, reminded a person that hope was always possible.

"Okay," she said. "Two for meals—"

"Three."

"Who's the third?"

"You."

"Oh. Of course." She'd hoped that was the case but didn't want to presume too much. "And these meals take place at what time?"

"We don't have a rigid schedule. I'm usually in the kitchen at five—"

"In the morning?" Horror sneaked into her voice before she could check it.

His brows winged up. "Yes. Is that a problem?"

"No, of course not." *Yes, a big one.* She wasn't a crack-of-dawn, early-riser type to begin with, but more distressing was that lately she wasn't always so bright-eyed and bushy-tailed even later in the morning. Then again, the afternoons and evenings often gave her trouble, too.

She fixed a competent look on her face, one she'd learned early on in business. Always project confidence. Never let on that you don't know the recipe. Smile and fake it.

"And supper time?"

"I'm usually back in by six. But you don't have to worry about me. I can get along fine. It's just Nikki that you have to take care of."

She gave him back one of the long, quiet looks he was so fond of giving her. "Did Aunt Lottie only fix meals for Nikki?"

He shook his head.

"There you go, then. Supper for three at six. Anything else? Special plans for the Fourth of July?"

"Yes. I'd forgotten. There's a picnic after church this Sunday and fireworks when it gets dark. Then…" He rubbed his brow. "What day does the actual holiday fall on?"

"Tuesday."

"Right. Lottie used to keep all those details straight for me."

"And now you have me." She hadn't meant the words to come out so suggestively.

Stony swallowed hard. "Tuesday the neighbors are getting together in the evening at Brewer's Saloon in town."

She glanced away, saw Nikki tiptoeing out of the stall, the cat no longer in her arms, the black Irish setter—her partner in crime—right on her heels.

She looked back at Stony and noticed that he'd seen the little girl, too.

"I ought to go investigate that, don't you think?"

"Probably. One of us should."

"I'll go. It's my job." She started to move away, then paused. "Is the picnic after church the kind where everyone brings a dish, or is each family responsible for their food?"

"I'm not sure."

He looked so confused she had to smile. "I'll find out and make sure that you show up with the right thing."

"We."

"Excuse me?"

"*We* show up. In a town like this, nobody misses

a get-together. If you're sticking around, I imagine they'll plan a welcoming social in your honor."

"For a housekeeper?"

"For anyone who comes to town, regardless of how long they plan to stay."

"I'll be staying awhile."

He studied her for several unnerving minutes. "I can't imagine why you'd be happy way out here on a ranch like this. We're not exactly a hopping metropolis."

"Maybe I'm not looking for a hopping metropolis."

"What are you looking for?"

She took a breath, wondered how she could answer him honestly without pushing, without blowing it. "A chance. A different direction."

He stepped forward, brushed a thumb over the fragile skin beneath her eye. "A chance to heal?"

She sucked in a breath. Did he know? Did he read her soul the way he read the horses? She put her hand over his, nearly told him what she wanted, what she needed.

Desperately.

"You see a lot, don't you?" she whispered.

He pulled his hand from hers as though he'd forgotten he'd been the one to touch first, as though he had no idea how his hand had gotten joined with hers in the first place.

"It's hard to miss those dark circles under your eyes."

She shrugged, bit her lower lip, was on the verge of blurting out her problems.

Not on the first day, Eden. Be patient.

"I'm fine."

It looked as if he intended to debate that statement. In the end he simply nodded. "Take it slow."

Chapter Three

When Eden was nervous or had a lot on her mind, she cooked. And although she'd been assigned by Vera Tillis—who was handling the food organization for the potluck—to fry up some chicken, Eden had also whipped up an apricot cake, a lemon soufflé, three dozen double-chocolate brownies, a marinated vegetable salad and a platter of deviled eggs.

It was a direct result of not being able to sleep the night before, of too many thoughts marching through her brain.

Even after several hours, the scent of baking still lingered on the air, and Eden felt the pull of lethargy from lack of rest. Not smart, she chided herself. Low hemoglobin levels were doing a fine job of zapping her energy. Adding insomnia to the list was guaranteed to knock her on her behind.

She grabbed a fistful of vitamins, downed them with some lukewarm tea, then turned, intending to wake Nikki and get her ready for church.

She gave a startled squeak when she saw Stony standing in the kitchen doorway. For such a big man, he was awfully quiet. Both verbally and on his feet.

His gaze skimmed over her broomstick skirt and button-front cotton shirt, then shifted to the array of food artfully arranged in bowls and on platters.

"Looks like you got double duty on the food assignments."

Eden sighed. "Actually I was only supposed to bring fried chicken. Then I found myself making a cake, and once I looked at it I realized it certainly wouldn't go far at a town celebration, so I made the soufflé, and then things kind of snowballed from there." She shrugged. "When it comes to cooking, I tend to get carried away."

"If it tastes any way near as good as it smells, it'll be gone in minutes."

"Do you think so?"

His brows lifted. "A caterer needing reassurance on her cooking?"

"Most of the time, no. I'm usually catering for clients and it's planned right down to the color and fold of the napkins. This is different." She fiddled with the round cake plate, realigned it with the soufflé. "Kind of like a new artist standing beside her work at her first gallery showing. It's personal." She wanted these people to like her.

She wanted Stony to like her.

"If you're wondering how your reviews will come in, I can tell you they'll be five-star."

"Without even tasting it?"

"I know the people. I know what I smell."

She chose a brownie off the platter, moved toward him and held it up to his lips. "I'm nervous. Aunt Lottie's shoes are hard to fill. Taste."

Stony opened his mouth, felt his stomach flip when she licked her lips, opening her mouth, too, unconsciously mimicking his moves. Her finger touched his lips, and his mind went blank.

"Well?"

She was waiting for approval. He had no idea what he'd eaten. "Delicious."

"Good. I feel better now."

It took every ounce of his control to step back from her. "I hope you had Vera put the cake mixes and supplies on my account."

"Shame on you. I don't use cake mixes."

"Oh."

She whirled back to him. "Why? Did it taste like I did? You weren't being truthful, were you?" She stared at the food laid out on the table, waiting to be wrapped up or packed in ice and loaded in the car, looking as though she wished she had time to start over.

"I'm always truthful, Eden."

The way he said her name made shivers go down her spine. He said it softly, subtly, distinctly, in that slow, deep voice. She was beginning to anticipate his mannerisms. A direct look, a pause as though weighing and choosing words.

She blinked. All that over the simple use of her name. She couldn't remember when she'd last been this nervous, and she was determined to cut it out.

She cleared her throat. "I should go wake Nikki."

"I did it on my way down."

"Then I'll make sure she's dressed."

"Did that, too."

Then what do you need me for? She didn't dare ask the question. She might not like the answer. And in truth, *she* was the one who needed *him*.

"Well, then. We know I can cook, so I'll get to

it." She held up a hand. "And don't even try to talk me out of it. Nothing's more embarrassing than growling stomachs in church." She took a carton of eggs out of the refrigerator and set them on the counter, then tied an apron around her waist. "Usually happens right during that silent pause between the last word of the prayer and 'amen.' Sit down." She paused, shot him a look. "Unless you've got something else to do?"

He sat at the table. "Already done. So when did you do all this cooking? You weren't up when I went out this morning."

"You went out?"

"The horses still like to eat, even on Sundays."

"Oh. Of course." With one hand she cracked eggs in a bowl, then slid a package of sausage in the skillet and grated some cheese. "I had trouble sleeping last night."

"Something wrong with the room?"

"Oh, no. It's perfect." From the refrigerator she took the pan of cinnamon rolls she'd also mixed up last night and popped them in the oven. "I guess it's being in a new place. Adjusting."

His direct look seemed to say that was a pretty lame excuse—especially given the way she'd zonked out and slept like the dead her first night here.

Thankfully, he didn't voice the apparent thought.

EDEN UNDERSTOOD why Aunt Lottie loved this town. The people were wonderfully warm and truly, genuinely delighted to welcome her.

As they laid out the food on long folding tables behind the church, Eden couldn't help but wonder

if Aunt Lottie had told any of the ladies her purpose
for coming to Shotgun Ridge. It seemed odd that
her aunt wouldn't have confided in somebody, that
a close-knit group like this wouldn't ferret out the
reason a longtime resident had up and left on vacation the way Lottie and Ray had.

Actually, Lottie and Ray were staying in Eden's
house in Dallas. They'd traded residences.

"This is a fine-looking spread. You bet."

Eden smiled at Ozzie Peyton. With a full head of
gray hair and eyes so blue they made a woman want
to stare, Ozzie looked a good ten years younger than
his seventy-something Stony had told her he was.

"Wait till you see the array of food Eden
brought," Iris Brewer said. Iris's husband, Lloyd,
who owned and operated Brewer's Saloon in town,
was one of the four cronies as the town affection-
ately called them. "She'll be stiff competition for
blue ribbons come time for the fair. I might even
have to hire her to spruce up the menu at Brewer's."

"Now, Iris," Ozzie said. "Your menu is just fine
the way it is. You bet. Besides, Eden here's gonna
have her hands full seeing to Stony and little Nikki.
You bet." He shook his head. "Craziest thing about
Carlotta up and leaving the way she done."

"Mmm," Eden murmured noncommittally.

"Her and Ray were about due for a vacation,
though. Told them so myself."

Eden's gaze whipped up to Ozzie's, and she felt
her cheeks fill with heat.

Ozzie Peyton knew why she was here. Did his
buddies know, too?

She looked quickly around. How many others
knew? Oh, she'd known these people would find out

sooner or later, small towns were notorious for their wildfire grapevine. She'd just hoped it would be later rather than sooner, that she'd have a chance to settle in, get to know them, try her best not to give the wrong impression.

Ozzie laid a hand on her shoulder, waited until Iris had moved farther down the table to arrange the desserts.

"Being the mayor and all, I'm pretty much up on everybody's comings and goings. But I got a strict rule about confidentiality." He drew out each syllable of the word. "You understand what I'm sayin' here?"

Eden felt a lump form in her throat and nodded.

"It'll be just fine, missy. You bet." He glanced around.

"And here comes old Stony now." Where a minute ago his voice was barely above a whisper, now it boomed. "Probably comin' to see how come I got my paws on his girl—uh, I mean, new housekeeper."

Having delivered his accidentally on-purpose slip, Ozzie clapped Stony on the shoulder and eased away. "The ladies could probably use a hand settin' up the rest of these tables. You boys ought to get over here and help. I'll just go herd Wyatt and Ethan this way."

Ozzie hurried off, but Stony didn't take his eyes off Eden. "You okay?"

"Yes, I'm fine. Why?" Her heart was pounding and she still hadn't truly settled on how she felt about the conversation she'd just had with Ozzie— or learning that Aunt Lottie had also had a conversation with him.

He took the pie out of her hands and set it on the table. "You've been going nonstop since we got here, and you're tired."

"I'm fine," she repeated.

He lightly touched her cheekbone, a butterfly caress that was gone before she could appreciate it. "It's not nice to fib. Especially this close to the church. Why don't you go take it easy for a while."

"For goodness' sake, I'm—"

He pressed his finger over her lips. In that instant, time seemed to stand still. She gazed into his whiskey-colored eyes, felt as though he was looking clear into her soul. She wished she could read him half as well as he seemed to read her.

Her heartbeat sped up, and her hands trembled. Yes, she was tired, but she was also energized by Stony's gentle touch, his probing, sensual look. Energized and filled with hope.

He was attracted to her.

Although, clearly, for some reason he didn't want to be.

Nearby, a sparkler glittered to life, and a child shrieked in glee, breaking the spell that seemed to have woven itself around them.

Stony dropped his hand, stepped back. "Iris, you women go sit down under the shade tree and enjoy the afternoon. I'll take care of the tables, here."

"Why thank you, Stony." Iris wiped her hands on a napkin and came around the long table to link arms with Eden. "You don't have to ask me twice. I see Ozzie's shooed Wyatt and Ethan this way, so we'll just leave you to it. Come on, Eden. Let's make a run for it before they change their minds."

Stony already had his back turned and was lifting

dishes out of the ice chest, making Eden wonder if she'd imagined that odd, charged moment between them.

"You've met Wyatt and Hannah Malone, haven't you?" Iris asked.

"Briefly, at church."

"Well, let me just catch you up on the gossip. My husband, Lloyd—much to my chagrin more often than not—is in cahoots with Ozzie, Henry and Vern. Henry owns the feed store in town, and you met Vern and Vera Tillis at the general store, right?"

"Yes."

"Anyway, the old coots cooked up a crazy idea and ran Wyatt's picture in a magazine advertising for a mail-order bride. Problem is, Wyatt didn't know about it."

Eden grinned. "That must have been uncomfortable."

"Yes, but I must say it was great fun. You see, Wyatt was married to my Becky, but we lost her and our grandson in an accident."

"Oh, I am sorry."

Iris patted Eden's hand. "Thank you, dear. As it turns out, I've gained an honorary daughter in Hannah, and grandchildren, as well, with Hannah's little Ian and the baby to come."

"Stony's talked about Ian. I'm told his Nikki is promised to Ian in about eighteen years time."

Iris laughed. "Wouldn't that be something. Then again, Dora and Ethan Callahan's little cherub might give Nikki a run for her money. Katie's just a bit over a year, but by the time they get grown, that won't be such a span."

"Sounds like Ian's going to be a busy young man if a few more little boys don't show up to take the pressure off."

"How right you are." Iris laughed gaily again. "If my husband and Ozzie Peyton have their way, there will be. It's a goal of theirs, you see, to bring women and babies to our town."

Eden felt a jolt of longing, felt the familiar squeezing of her heart.

To distract herself she asked, "So what other shenanigans have they pulled?" *Besides helping Aunt Lottie concoct a scheme and dragging Eden right into it.*

"They had a bachelor auction. With our town playboy as their target."

"Ethan Callahan?" Nikki had imparted that little tidbit yesterday. Eden had been surprised to hear a five-year-old describing her uncle that way.

"One and the same. I tell you what, that boy didn't know what hit him when the preacher's daughter showed up and presented him with a baby."

"Yikes. He got a preacher's daughter pregnant?"

"No. It was Dora's best friend—who died tragically, I'm afraid. You'll have to get Dora to tell you all about it sometime. She's a spitfire, that one. And just perfect for Ethan."

"This bachelor auction...were all the guys in town involved?"

"You mean was Stony there?"

"Not that it makes a difference," she said quickly. "I'm just his housekeeper and Nikki's nanny." *So far.*

Iris gave her a soft, chiding smile and shook her

head. "I still don't quite know how he slipped out on that one. We blinked, and next thing we knew, he'd skipped out of town with Grant and Clay Callahan."

For some reason Eden was glad he hadn't gone on a date with some woman who was looking for a husband.

Iris patted Eden's hand and unlinked their arms. "You rest here on this blanket, love."

"Why does everyone keep telling me to rest? Do I look like the walking dead or something?" If there was one thing Eden hated, it was admitting to a weakness.

"Of course you don't. But you've made a long trip from Dallas and..." Her words faltered. "Naturally Lottie spoke of you and told us where you live," she explained quickly.

But Eden realized that Iris was another one Lottie had evidently confided in. Eden had told the other woman she'd driven from Texas. She hadn't mentioned which town.

This was awkward.

She eased down on the blanket she'd spread earlier, picking at the burrs that clung to it. The grass beneath was soft and green, shaded from the July sun by a leafy cottonwood. A few feet away a creek bubbled over smooth rocks, the sound soothing, making her realize she was indeed a bit tired.

To the right she could still see the white church with its steeple reaching toward the heavens. Here there was peace. Here a soul could heal. Surely that would make a difference.

Carrying a plate laden with food, Stony eased down on the blanket beside her. Eden watched several of the single women following him with their eyes, giving him covert looks.

And as astonishing as it seemed, Stony genuinely didn't notice.

"So, with all these new women showing up in town, have you, uh, thought about dating any of them?"

"Not interested."

"You can't tell me none of these women have approached you."

"Don't imagine they're interested."

"Are you kidding?"

He looked up, directly into her eyes. "No."

How in the world could this man not realize the effect he had on the female population?

His utter masculinity, combined with his quiet compassion, drew women like bees to pollen. Anyone with a set of eyes in their head could see it. Provided they were looking. Which Stony apparently wasn't.

She watched him tug at his hat, tip it lower on the right side. When she turned more fully to face him, he shifted, too. It was ever so subtle, but she noticed his self-conscious effort to hide his scar.

The man actually believed he was ugly.

She might have pursued the subject, but excited children's voices interrupted.

"Eden, come catch the tadpoles with us," Nikki begged, skidding to a halt next to the blanket, little Ian Malone at her side. Both children's faces were shiny with sweat.

"Ah, fishing for tadpoles. My favorite sport."

Stony nearly swallowed his tongue when she stood and hooked her thumbs in the waistband of her flowing, crinkly skirt. Before he could form a thought or an objection—or even an encouragement—she'd peeled the skirt down her hips and stepped out of it.

Thankfully, she wore a pair of beige shorts beneath.

He noticed a couple of the other men were watching the impromptu striptease, and he scowled at them.

"Make you nervous?" she asked, looking down at him with a devilish sparkle in her eyes.

He couldn't figure out if she was teasing him or genuinely flirting with him. Odd that he could normally read the expressions and body language of most people, yet with Eden he had trouble.

"Me and about five other men here. Including the preacher."

Her gaze whipped up. Now *this* expression he could read. Horror. Embarrassment.

He started to grin, felt his scar pull and settled on a half smile. "It's what you get."

Her brow arched. "One of these days I'm going to get the whole smile out of you instead of just half." She kicked off her sandals and took Nikki's hand, allowing the child to pull her toward the creek.

"Are we going to fry up these tadpoles in the skillet, or bake them stuffed with mushrooms and a pinch of tarragon?" he heard her ask. Nikki's delighted laugh floated back.

And Stony told himself he was *not* going to consider any sensual possibilities with regard to Eden Williams, no matter how much that magnolia-blossom drawl got to him.

She was beautiful.

And she was temporary.

Suddenly bored with his own company, he went to join the circle of men who'd congregated by the food tables. Like vultures waiting to pounce, the curiosity on his friends' faces was blatant.

His gut tightened and he shot them a scowl that had them backing off, not putting voice to their questions and taunts. He'd been friends with these guys since they were young boys. They knew when it was prudent to remain silent, and most of the time they actually respected those boundaries.

When dusk turned to dark, the men gathered in a cleared section of land and argued over the fairest way to decide which one of them got to be the pyromaniac who lit the fuses. They went through this every year, and Stony was happy to step aside and leave them to it.

Fire still gave him uncomfortable shivers of flashbacks. Nikki, too, was apprehensive, but too young to understand why.

He knew it was important to get to her before the real light show of sparks began.

He found her on the blanket sitting between Eden's knees, her back resting against Eden's chest. The sight momentarily halted his progress.

Nikki had never known a mother—or remembered, at least. She had plenty of honorary grandmothers, but sometimes he wondered if the day would come when she truly ached for more. More than he could provide.

The sight of Eden with his daughter touched him, made his yearning mind create scenarios he had no business dwelling on.

He eased down on the blanket beside them. "Finished entertaining with your guitar?'' He'd seen her earlier with an avid audience, catering mainly to the children, doing her best to keep them laughing. And she'd done a fine job.

He hadn't trusted himself to join in.

''We singed about the beer, Daddy, and forgot the milk.''

''It was a slip,'' Eden defended.

''Mmm, hmm,'' he murmured.

''And then we did the ants and the fishies.'' The first burst of fire popped high in the sky, and Nikki flinched.

''Oh, doll baby, did that catch you off guard?'' Eden smoothed a hand over Nikki's forehead, pushing sweaty bangs back with each sweep. She felt the child snuggle closer and automatically tightened her hold, offering security. ''Isn't it pretty?''

Another vivid ball of color burst in the sky, showering a kaleidoscope of mesmerizing embers that fell like the sweeping branches of a weeping willow.

Nikki nodded and held out her hand for Stony. When he took the little girl's palm in his, there was no way to avoid having the back of his arm and hand resting on Eden's thigh.

She tried to be nonchalant about it but wondered if he could hear the gallop of her heart. It pulsed loudly in her own ears. She tried to tell herself to calm down, to remind herself that she always went all soft and mushy when she saw those calendars with pictures of men and children on them. This was the same thing. Anyone would be touched by the sight of Nikki's tiny hand resting in Stony's wide palm.

Despite the noise and show, Nikki fell asleep against Eden's chest.

"Why don't we lay her down," Stony suggested and helped her shift and lower the child to the blanket. Her apple-shaped cheeks and sweet lips had remnants of mustard and chocolate on them. She'd played hard today and now would sleep hard.

Eden turned her head at the same time Stony did. Their shoulders touched and she went still, raising her gaze to his. A thrill shot through her at the intensity of his gaze, the way his eyes shifted from hers to her mouth, then back.

Hardly aware of the movement, Eden leaned closer. She could feel the warmth of his breath on her lips and wanted in the worst way to have him make that final, critical move, to know what his kiss would feel like.

"We're missing the show." His voice was deep and spellbinding, tense with control.

"Are we? I hadn't noticed." Reluctance radiated from him so strongly she imagined she could touch it, yet she could see the burning desire in his whiskey-brown eyes. She didn't understand the contrast, the hesitation.

She wanted to scream when he drew back.

"This isn't a good idea," he said quietly. "People will talk."

She nodded even as her gaze clung. She imagined people would be talking, anyway. It was just a matter of time.

WHEN EDEN ANSWERED THE PHONE the next morning, the caller didn't even identify herself.

"Well?"

"Hello, Aunt Lottie. Are you taking good care of my plants?" Eden pictured Lottie and Ray in her modest three-bedroom home just outside of Dallas, with its killer kitchen and fabulous yard. She loved that home, the quiet, tree-shaded street, the expansive lawns and raised porches where neighbors often stopped by for coffee and muffins or whatever Eden had fresh from the oven.

Purchasing that house had been a measure of her business success, a sign that Garden of Eden Catering was flourishing after years of hard work and sacrifice.

"Your plants are thriving and wonderful. Although I must say, I don't understand some of the art on the walls, dear."

Eden smiled. "It's music memorabilia, Aunt Lottie." From Marilyn Monroe to the Beatles to the Dixie Chicks, she collected classy prints of famous and not-so-famous musicians. She imagined, though, that her aunt was referring to a couple of the wilder posters where the band members looked more like Halloween characters than entertainers.

"Yes, well, despite that grim-faced bunch hanging over the sofa in the den, you have a beautiful home. I know your parents must be so proud of your success."

"You haven't told Mother, have you?" As much as Eden loved her parents, they had a tendency to meddle in her life, and still thought after thirty-four years that they knew what was best for her. If Beverley Williams found out the risk Eden was taking, she'd be on her like ducks on a june bug.

"No, hon, I haven't. Your mom's my best friend,

but I know what she's like—though she's truly well-meaning, you know.''

"I know. I hate all this deceit, Aunt Lottie. It's not me. I've never lied in my life—well, maybe once or twice as a kid, but—''

"Have you actually lied, hon?''

"By omission.''

"Your parents will understand once they realize the urgency.''

"I was talking about Stony, as well.''

There was a pause on the line. "So what did he say?''

"That's just it. I haven't asked him yet.''

"Why in the world not?''

"Aunt Lottie, this isn't exactly something you blurt out, you know.'' With the phone cord wrapped around her finger, she turned...and nearly fainted.

Stony was standing behind her, unashamedly listening.

Her heart surged so hard she actually saw stars.

"I've got to go,'' she whispered. Like an inferno, the heat of chagrin drenched her. "Talk to you soon.'' She hung up the phone, rubbed her damp palms on the seat of her jeans and turned to face the music. Or Stony, rather.

"So, has Lottie recovered from her stress?''

She nodded. His gaze was fixed so steadily on her it took every bit of her will not to squirm.

"Thought so.'' He took off his hat, bounced it gently against his thigh. Although his voice was achingly pleasant, he was clearly annoyed. "Don't you think it's time you told me what's really going on? Why you're here?''

Think, Eden. Don't blow it. She opened her mouth, felt her heart nearly pound out of her chest.

"I need to have a baby." Adrenaline shot through her so fast she had to grab the countertop for support. It felt as though her lungs had collapsed, and try as she might, she couldn't seem to draw in enough air to chase away the dizziness.

She'd told Aunt Lottie she couldn't just blurt it out, yet that's exactly what she'd done.

And there was no turning back now.

When he didn't react, didn't move so much as an eyelash, she tried again, her voice and hands trembling with fear and embarrassment…and a quiet desperation that squared her shoulders and lifted her chin, gave her courage.

"I want you to get me pregnant."

In the silence that followed they could have heard an ant sneeze.

Stony blinked, stared, then jammed his hat on his head, and without a single word or change in expression, he turned and walked out the door.

Chapter Four

Eden stared at the kitchen door, her heart in her throat. Well, what had she expected?

They hadn't even kissed and she'd asked him to have sex with her. It was little wonder that he'd stared at her as if she'd lost her mind and walked out.

She closed her eyes, wondering what to do now. He was her hope. Yet his reaction just now had all but extinguished that hope.

Folding her arms, she hugged her waist as though protecting herself, as though the pressure could keep the panic from spilling out of her like a river of blood.

Apt analogy, Eden.

Her period was due to start in a couple of days. Her plan had been to take the first two weeks to settle in, to form a bond with Stony, and by the time they'd both agreed they couldn't wait a moment more before making love, it would most likely be her time of ovulation. It hadn't really crossed her mind that Stony—or any man for that matter— would turn down an offer of sex.

It sounded so calculating now. So sexist. Why hadn't it before?

When the kitchen door opened again, she jumped.

Stony stood at the threshold for a long moment, then took off his hat and closed the door.

He'd only been gone a few minutes, which meant he couldn't have gotten much farther than the back porch before he'd turned around.

He was a difficult man to read. So silent. So watchful. He didn't waste words on chitchat.

And Eden suddenly wished he would.

Anything to hold back time. Anything to keep him from escorting her off his property, dashing her dreams.

"Why?" His voice was quiet yet reverberated around the room like the report of a pistol. Most people would have automatically asked her to repeat herself.

Not Stony, though. He'd heard correctly the first time. Nothing got past him. He just took his time about processing, sifted through the facts, then asked for further clarification.

Odd how she could discern certain qualities in him, yet was unable to read his expressions, to get even a hint of what was going through his mind.

It made her feel even more vulnerable that she couldn't.

He was still waiting for her explanation, and now that the time was at hand, Eden didn't know where to start. She thought she'd had it all worked out in her head—that an attraction between them could have sparked and ignited, and from there, simply followed the natural, typical, *expected* progression and conclusion.

Sexual intimacy.

She took a breath. "Where's Nikki?" She'd been with Stony earlier.

"Demone's giving her a riding lesson."

"Isn't she a little young for—"

"Eden."

She swallowed. Nodded. "Maybe we should sit." At least, she should. Otherwise she might fall. But Stony merely moved across the kitchen, crossed his arms over his broad chest and leaned against the counter.

Eden didn't want to be at the disadvantage of having him tower over her, so she stayed on her feet and paced.

"I want to have a baby, but I have a medical condition called adenomyosis—endometriosis of the uterus muscle." She glanced at him, but his expression hadn't changed. "It's a female thing, but it's not contagious or anything," she assured quickly.

Still no change in his expression.

She sighed and looked out the kitchen window, twisting her fingers together until her knuckles appeared bloodless. With her gaze focused on two butterflies flying in acrobatic circles around a pansy, she deliberately untangled her fingers and gripped the lip of the sink. Her knees were shaking so hard she wasn't certain she could stay upright.

"I don't imagine those technical terms make much sense to you. Basically, I've got a condition that causes me to have heavy periods which in turn causes fairly severe anemia."

Essentially, Dr. Amies had said, she was nearly bleeding to death once a month.

"The doctor wants to operate…perform a hysterectomy.'' Just saying the word made her want to sit down and bawl. ''But I want children, a child, at least. I want the experience of carrying a baby in my womb if at all possible.''

She swallowed, could hardly speak above a whisper. She had no idea if he could hear her, if he was even listening. A bead of water clinging to the curve of the sink slid down the porcelain like a tear.

''I've only got six months to try and make that happen.''

She felt his hands on her shoulders and jumped.

''Come sit down, Eden.''

Tears stung the back of her eyes at the gentleness of his voice. He had every right to be angry because she was here under false pretenses, had essentially lied to him—albeit by omission. Yet instead of sharpness, he spoke to her as though she were a cherished friend—or lover.

The emotions crowding inside her felt as though, any minute now, they'd break through the dam of her control. And if she allowed that, where would she be? She couldn't feel sorry for herself. She had to take action. It's how she'd always conducted her life.

He turned her and led her to a chair at the kitchen table. She was grateful when he sat down opposite her, almost as if he'd understood her need to be on an equal footing.

She brushed a long strand of hair back off her face and gave him a tentative smile. ''I didn't mean to spring this on you.''

''What did you mean to do?''

Her shoulders lifted, and she gave a nervous laugh. ''At least wait until we'd kissed.''

The attempt to lighten the moment fell flat. Eden couldn't remember a time when she'd ever felt so nervous…or foolish. But she'd started this communication, and she had to see it through. Honestly.

"I thought if there was chemistry between us, and we had the convenience of being under the same roof, we'd just let nature take its course."

"And is there?"

"What?"

"Chemistry."

His direct look made her squirm. For some reason she had the feeling he was holding his breath, that her answer was vitally important to him. "I think there is," she said softly, leaving herself totally vulnerable. He hadn't reciprocated by assuring her he felt the same way.

"So then what? You take advantage of an…attraction, we hit the sheets, then once you get what you came for, you leave as mysteriously as you arrived…and never bother to tell me I'm a father?"

"No! That would have never happened. Honestly, Stony. This is difficult for me, this conversation about…my personal flaws, female things. Especially since we don't really know each other."

His brows lifted as if to say, *Exactly, yet you just asked me to have sex with you.* She was making a mess of the whole thing.

"What I'm trying to say is that when a couple is intimate, it's just easier to discuss this stuff. And I would have. When we were…more familiar. I wouldn't have left and not told you if I was pregnant."

But the reminder made her realize she hadn't truly thought through that part of her wild request. The ticking of the clock had caused her to act rashly, had all but blinded her to everything except the immediate goal.

To have a baby growing in her womb while the possibility still existed.

The intensity of his amber gaze never wavered as he studied her, searched her face for the truth. Finally, he nodded and took a long breath that expanded his chest and pulled at the snaps on his shirt.

"This was your idea?"

She didn't meet his eyes. "Uh, actually, Aunt Lottie sort of suggested it."

"And you jumped with both feet?"

She looked back at him. "No. I thought she was nuts."

"Evidently not too nuts."

"I'm thirty-four, Stony, and I've never had a one-night stand. I've had a few committed relationships that didn't work out, but I've never taken sex lightly. I still don't. But when a person is feeling desperate, suggestions, even ones that are way out there or slightly iffy, have a way of sounding right, of making sense." She paused, swallowed. "And I'm feeling desperate."

He swore, raked a hand through his mahogany hair. "Isn't there some other treatment for this…"

"We've tried. The last effort was a drug called depo-provera to control my…uh, cycle." She saw his eyes skitter away the same time hers did. This wasn't getting any easier, or any less embarrassing, for either of them. She didn't have brothers, and she'd been brought up in the Southern tradition and taught that ladies didn't talk about delicate subjects in polite company. "I couldn't tolerate the side effects of the medication."

"What about artificial insemination?"

"I don't have that kind of money. Or the time to chance it not working."

He lifted a brow. "Six months is six months. What's the difference?"

Her face flamed with heat, but she lifted her chin. "A big one to my way of thinking. In a healthy, committed relationship between a man and a woman, they normally make love fairly often, thereby increasing the odds considerably if a person is trying for a baby. Twenty-five times or so a month is obviously better math than a one-time shot."

"Only twenty-five?"

"Give or take. I factored in time off for monthly female—" She stopped, glared at him, not sure if he'd been teasing or sarcastic. With his solemn countenance it was hard to tell.

"So, why me?"

"Because Aunt Lottie recommended you." She took a breath, shook her head. "That sounds really bad, I know." But through her aunt's glowing description of Stony, Eden's hope had begun to blossom. Desperate, at the end of her rope, with the clock ticking away her fate, she'd needed to cling to something, been willing to take the biggest, perhaps even the most foolish risk of her life—to leave a thriving business and life she adored and to put her trust in a man she'd never met, simply on the strength of her aunt's recommendation....

And on a powerful, giddy reaction to a photograph.

It had come in the mail, the brown envelope

stamped with Aunt Lottie's return address. With sticky bread dough still clinging to her hands, she'd slid the single photograph out of its jacket and felt an immediate flutter in her stomach, a shortness of breath.

It was those eyes, the color of fine scotch with drizzles of molasses. Intense, yet gentle somehow.

Eyes that held the same expression right now.

And suddenly, without understanding how, Eden knew he was going to turn her down.

"I don't think this is going to work, Eden. I'm not the right man."

Panic seized her. "But you are. I'm here. This is perfect. You're perfect."

He shook his head. "There are plenty of other men in town."

"But I'm already here," she repeated. How could she convince him when even now she realized the rashness and illogic of her impulsive plan? She had to try, though.

"I'm working for you, Stony, living under the same roof. Don't you see? It's perfect. I've screwed up my courage to ask you—and despite what you might think, this isn't easy for me." Never mind that she'd jumped the gun and blurted rather than asked. Her objective was out in the open. And if it sounded as though she was begging, so be it. She had no pride. Only a fiercely coveted dream.

"I've put my business and my life on hold. I can't go back to town now—besides, Aunt Lottie's in Texas and you still need someone to care for Nikki."

"Eden—"

She reached across the table and gripped his forearm. "I'm running out of time, Stony. If I went back to town, what would you have me do? Take out an ad? Hang out a shingle on the door inviting men to come on in?"

He scowled. "Don't be ridiculous."

"Well?"

"Why didn't you choose someone in Texas? Wasn't there anyone you were seeing?"

"No. I told you I've been busy." She dropped her forehead into her palm. "When the doctor gave me the ultimatum, I confess I panicked—which isn't like me at all. I haven't gone out on a date in four months—"

"What the hell's wrong with those Texans?" he muttered, then looked as though he wished he could snatch the words back.

She felt the beginning of a smile chase away a bit of the anxiety. "Thank you," she said softly. "That's the nicest compliment I've had in a long time."

His look suggested he didn't believe that for a minute.

But the fact that it was true made her want to weep, brought her back to the pressing dilemma that was already two weeks closer to the deadline.

Fourteen fewer days to try for a baby.

"Actually, the availability of decent guys is pretty slim—at least the ones I've come in contact with lately. Seems they're just out to have a good time, or they're married—a minor detail they neglect to mention. That's not the kind of man I'd consider approaching to have a baby with."

Stony raised his brows, and Eden realized she was making a bigger mess of this explanation—and that her motivation was sounding thinner and wilder by the moment.

But she had to press on, had to make him understand.

"All my life I've always known exactly where I was headed and how I'd get there. I don't think I consciously knew how important children and family were to me until I was faced with the possibility of not being able to have them. I'd always planned to marry someday and have a bunch of kids, but I'd put first things first. I've spent these past ten years building a successful business, never realizing that 'someday' might be snatched from me. I've controlled my destiny with solid planning and a ton of faith. What I can't control is my body, and it's suddenly decided to fail me." She scooped a strand of hair behind her ear.

"Now I'm racing against time, and my choices are to bleed to death or to have surgery that will prevent the possibility of ever having a baby."

"Damn it, is your life in jeopardy?"

She hadn't meant to blurt that out. And she refused to believe it. "I'm taking vitamins to counteract the anemia…and it only happens once a month. But I can't keep it up forever." She looked him straight in the eyes. "Please, Stony."

Stony pinched the bridge of his nose, his mind whirling. Now he understood the fleeting shadows he'd seen in her eyes when she'd first come, the faint discoloration of the fragile skin beneath those eyes, the uncanny sense that she was hiding something.

Now that he knew her true agenda and the reasons

behind it, he couldn't help responding, wanting to protect her, to make it right.

She was too young and vibrant to have the possibility of family taken from her.

He'd seen her with Nikki and Ian, wading in the creek, trapping minnows with a kitchen strainer, laughing and frolicking, passing out hugs and healing kisses when a knee got scraped. Then later, strumming her guitar, entertaining the children and neighbors with her songs, holding Nikki close when the day had grown long, arms tightening when fireworks had caused Nikki's little heart to beat like the wings of a frightened bird.

Eden Williams would be a great mother.

And it certainly wouldn't be any hardship on his part to oblige her in her plea.

From the moment he'd set eyes on her he'd been hard. He would have given half the Thoroughbreds on his farm just to kiss her, to feel her body against his, to pretend for just a while that he wasn't a big ox of a guy with hands the size of mitts and a mug that could double as a mask on Halloween…that he was a man who could attract a beautiful woman like Eden.

But he wasn't that kind of guy. Paula had shown him that quite clearly and definitely, to the tune of one million dollars.

Yet here was Eden, offering him the equivalent of every man's fantasy—with no strings attached.

And therein lay one of his biggest problems.

"I've got a daughter to think about, Eden. I can't conduct an affair with an impressionable child in the house."

The desolation that came over her nearly scraped

him raw. Her pale cheeks went even more ashen as understanding and acceptance registered.

"I didn't think," she whispered, the agony in her voice almost too much for him to bear.

He reached across the table and touched the back of her hand, feeling awkward as all get-out—even more so than usual. It was hard to remember that she was basically just using him.

The back door burst open, startling them both.

Hannah Malone made a grab for her son, but Ian skipped right into the kitchen behind Nikki, both kids frolicking like mischievous puppies.

"I'm sorry." Hannah stopped, glanced from Stony to Eden. "I should have called. I'm interrupting."

"No, it's fine." Eden popped up out of the chair, her gaze clinging for a bare instant on Hannah's straining, pregnant stomach. "Let me just get you something to drink." Her eyes were bright, and though a dimple creased her cheek, Stony noticed the slight tremble at the corner of her smile before she turned away to open the refrigerator.

Damn it.

"No, really, Eden, I can't stay." Hannah glanced at Stony, the expression on her wholesome face bland, the curiosity in her eyes anything but. "I just took a chance and came by on my way from town—actually I buckled under pressure. Ian wanted Nikki to come home with us to play, so I thought I'd stop and ask."

"Please, Daddy?" Nikki hop-skipped in a circle, pulling Stony's hand. Rosie sat beside her and barked as though adding her approval. "The billy goat ate Hannah's garden and we gotta go help her fix it.''

Stony glanced at Hannah. "Again? I thought Wyatt put up a fence to keep that from happening."

"Yes, well, *someone* left the little gate open." She cut her gaze to her four-year-old son, who was busy petting Rosie's head, oblivious that he was being talked about.

"Act'cally," Nikki said solemnly, her round little cheeks puffing out when she smacked her lips together. "Ian left it open, but Hannah's not mad at him. And the beetles are havin' their supper on Hannah's strawberries and I gotta get 'em 'cuz she's a'scared of 'em."

Stony's lips twitched, and Hannah looked sheepish but resigned.

"I'm making headway with the animals," Hannah said laughingly in her own defense. "But the bugs are still a bit of a trial."

"I'm sure they are." The entire town had rallied behind Hannah when she'd relocated from California to Montana, longing to fulfill her dream of being a rancher's wife—and scared to death of anything with fur or four legs.

"Can I, Daddy?"

"Yeah, can her?" Ian begged.

Stony ruffled both kids' hair. "Okay, but—"

The children's happy shrieks drowned out any instructions or admonitions he might have given. Realizing he'd be wasting his breath, anyway, he shook his head. "Go ahead and get your stuff, Nik."

"Yeah! I got a new backpack, Ian. Come and see." The kids took off at a run with Rosie on their heels.

"Might as well sit," Eden suggested to Hannah, smiling softly. "By the time Nikki takes everything out of the bag for Show and Tell and puts it back in again, it'll be a good fifteen minutes. Trust me, she insisted I admire it, too." She set a plate laden with fat sticky buns oozing melted brown sugar and plump walnuts on the table, along with a pitcher of tea. "It's herbal," she said, her gaze resting fleetingly on Hannah's belly.

"Oh, my gosh, those smell heavenly. Never mind that I'm big as a cow, I simply don't have any willpower. This baby's either going to crave sweets like mad or hate them." She bit into the roll and closed her eyes in ecstasy. "Eden, you're a genius. Anytime you want to come take over my kitchen, you'll be welcome."

Stony met Eden's quick gaze. Although she immediately looked away, he thought he knew what had crossed her mind. There wouldn't be much reason to stay here if she couldn't accomplish her objective within her six month time frame.

To get pregnant.

By him.

His heart thumped against his ribs. Wasn't that just his lot in life? Women who only wanted something from him? Who wouldn't stay? He thought he'd resigned himself to that reality, that it didn't bother him, that he no longer yearned.

He'd been kidding himself.

He wanted a family. A complete family. Husband-wife-mom-dad-child—or children.

If he agreed to her proposition, and she *did* become pregnant, could she be persuaded to stay?

He put away that thought. The last thing he wanted was anyone feeling obligated to be with him.

But the other thoughts—the crazy, impossible ones running around in his head about happy family units—were making his gut twist.

And, he thought, moving a step closer to Eden's chair, the bittersweet longing on Eden's face that she couldn't quite hide when she looked at Hannah's stomach was tearing him up.

The kids came bounding down the stairs, and Eden stood to wrap up the rest of the buns. "Take these home with you, Hannah."

"Oh, I can't. Stony will want—"

"I have plenty more." Eden gave a shrug and a small smile. "Some people pace when they think. I bake."

"And keep a body like that?"

"I've got good genes."

"Lucky you. Ready, kids?"

Nikki kissed Stony, then tugged Eden down to treat her to the same.

"Be good, sugar," Eden said, automatically brushing Nikki's bangs back out of her eyes.

A loving action a mother would do.

Stony looked away, feeling as though he'd been kicked in the gut by a mustang. He snapped his fingers for Rosie, who obediently trotted over and sat next to his side, even though she adopted a hound dog look because she hadn't been invited to go along. They watched as Hannah loaded the kids in her white minivan, then eased herself behind the wheel, her stomach nearly pressing against the steering wheel.

"She'll either have to put the seat back and grow

longer legs, or give up driving,'' Eden remarked, waving to the kids as Hannah maneuvered the van out of the circular driveway and down the lane.

Stony rested a hand on her shoulder and felt her tense. She looked up at him and gave him a smile, a smile that held both a question and an apology.

He understood what it was like to want something so desperately. He'd felt those clawing emotions as a kid when he'd towered over his classmates, suffered the taunts and the name calling—Hulk, behemoth, freak. *You're too ugly to get a home or be adopted.*

He'd wanted so badly to be normal, to look like everyone else, had prayed for it, at the time not realizing that one day the other guys would begin to catch up. That one day his grandmother would find him, that she hadn't thrown him away, that he would once again have a home and the love that had been so tragically snatched from him.

He stared at his big hand gently cupping Eden's slender shoulder, noted the contrast. He'd almost killed a guy with these hands and the reminder still made his gut clench.

He'd learned to ignore the stupid taunts directed at him, but a slur against his grandmother had erupted in a blood-red rage so swift he hadn't thought twice about letting his fist fly. He could still hear the solid sound of his knuckles connecting with flesh and bone. He'd only thrown one punch, but that's all it had taken.

The scope of the strength he possessed had frightened him, that and the fact that he was actually capable of truly harming someone.

From that day, he'd made it his daily goal to come

to terms with his size and his looks, to put away his temper. Grandma had told him he needed to learn balance, to watch and listen. If he looked deeply, he would see that the meanness of others had roots, that someone had trampled their self-esteem, and that kindness begets kindness—the same principle he used time and again on the horses, particularly the ones who were difficult to handle.

So he knew about yearning. In a different way, perhaps, but the same, nonetheless.

He looked down at Eden, drawn to the shadows in her eyes, compelled to erase them, telling himself to tread carefully, that no matter what, he wouldn't trap her.

Still, against all reason, he wanted to be Eden Williams's savior knight.

She let out a sigh that matched the weariness in her eyes. As though there hadn't been an interruption in their conversation, she said, "It's okay, Stony. I understand. This was a crazy idea to begin with, and I apologize for putting us both in an awkward position. I'll call Aunt Lottie and see how soon she can come home."

Her smile was brave; her voice, chipper. That he could see right through both made his heart ache.

"I have to warn you, they might balk at cutting their trip short. Even though they weren't strictly honest with you, this really is a vacation for them. They'd planned a kind of reunion with my parents and some of their other friends, but I'll see what I can do," she said brightly.

Too brightly.

When she stepped away from him, something inside him gave way, something he couldn't...or maybe *wouldn't* define.

He stopped her with a hand on her arm. "Marry me."

Chapter Five

It was Eden's turn to go mute. She stared at Stony, heard the whinny of horses outside, the pounding of hooves as trainers put the beautiful creatures through their paces.

"Excuse me?"

"I understand what you need," he said quietly. "But because of the circumstances, Nikki mainly, that's the only way I can see something like this working."

"Marriage?" Her head was suddenly spinning.

"With stipulations."

She swallowed, continued to gape at him. "Of course." Almost immediately she shook her head, held up a hand. "Wait a minute. What am I saying? There's no 'of course.'" Evidently, irrational behavior was contagious. And though she was the least likely of the two, someone had to be reasonable.

"They're necessary."

"What? Oh, stipulations…yes. But I meant marriage." She hadn't counted on permanence—just a baby. She was thoroughly taken by surprise and off balance. "Stony, I have a house and a business in Dallas. And a partner."

He gave a slow nod. "That's why I said stipulations. You've given yourself six months, obviously intending to spend them here in Montana. Fine. We'll give the marriage six months. If you're not pregnant by then, we'll call it quits."

She rubbed her forehead where a headache throbbed with a consistent dull pain. "And if I am?"

"Your choice. The door will still be open. I'll want rights as far as the child goes, though."

"Yes, of course." Her heartbeat stuttered, and her brain went into fast rewind. "What kind of rights? I mean, I never intended for you to pay child support or anything."

"If you have my baby, I'll pay child support." His statement was resolute, brooked no argument.

Although his attitude was commendable—the world would be a much better place if more men adopted the same one—Eden felt a slight niggling of unease.

"I'd want to see my son or daughter, have him know who I am. You can choose the schedule and how often, but the main stipulation's nonnegotiable."

She rested her hand on his arm. "I feel the same, Stony. That's one of the reasons I didn't pursue the clinical approach. It's important to me to know the father of my child. And I want my baby to know his or her father. That's how I'd always imagined it…in a perfect world, that is. Before…well, you know." If she'd had the luxury to wait for love and marriage. If the clock wasn't ticking.

He nodded. "I'd need my attorney to draft some papers, which of course will include clauses to protect *your* assets, as well."

"Oh." She fluttered a hand, a bit flustered. "I trust you."

"You don't know me."

"That's an odd thing to say after you've just offered marriage."

He shrugged. "It's true."

"You're right. And smart. Thank you for having a care for my protection. My mother's a judge—municipal court. She'd have fined me for stupidity if the code existed." Eden smiled. "I confess I'm a little muddled right now. I've never been married before."

"I have."

She gaped at him. "You have? Aunt Lottie never said anything."

"Why should she? It's old news. But you get my point now."

Yes, she got the point. Aunt Lottie had told her about Stony's personality, his gentleness, his uncanny ability to charm horses, his dedication as a father. She'd sent a photograph as further enticement. But that was the extent of it. Now that she thought about it, Aunt Lottie had never offered personal details, had never breached Stony's confidences.

Eden did not know Stony Stratton.

She only knew she had a powerful attraction to him. He made her tremble, and he made her ache in an elemental, carnal way.

But marriage? Could she do it?

She'd waited thirty-four years to do it right, had held on to the fairy-tale fantasies about love, marriage and family, even though she'd chosen to pursue career and financial stability first. That was the proper way to do things, she'd thought, the smart way.

Oh, she'd gone through the years of despairing that she'd ever marry, fearing that she'd end up an old maid. She'd watched her friends from high school settle down to husband, home, kids and car-pools, and had suffered through a gut-wrenching, demeaning period in life when she'd looked at every man with an eye toward getting him down the matrimonial aisle.

The worst had been when Carrie had gotten married. They were best friends—and partners in business now—and had always done things together.

Thankfully, Eden had come to her senses, learned to be patient, to be comfortable with who she was and to respect her goals. To fulfill her career and financial aspirations first, trusting that when she was mature enough, the right man would come into her life, a man who would love her and she him, in return. A man with whom she would share friendship as well as the kind of deep and abiding love that would overcome life's obstacles and carry them through until death would part them.

So, could she do this? Set aside her ideals of marriage and happily ever after? Could she enter into this sacred institution knowing up front that it could never work, that in fact it was predetermined to end in six months' time?

Because it *couldn't* work, even if she wanted it to. Her life and family were in Texas, more than fifteen hundred miles away.

And the man proposing marriage didn't love her.

Cramps tightened her belly, low in her abdomen,

sending a wave of nausea through her. She fought the weakness.

Just like she intended to fight it until the very last moment, until there was no longer any hope.

But right this minute there *was* hope.

And Stony Stratton was offering it…or agreeing, rather, with minor—major, she amended—alterations.

"Are you sure about this, Stony?"

"It's your decision."

That wasn't an answer. But she wanted a baby more than anything. She wanted to try.

With Stony, she realized.

Which meant agreeing to his conditions.

"When did you have in mind…to get married?"

"The sooner the better. Chances are good that Lottie didn't keep this plan to herself," he said. "All she'd need to do is tell one person, and the whole town would know in a matter of hours. Which means they're already speculating, wondering if we've started trying for this baby of ours."

His words and his steady look made her blush. The curse of her auburn hair color, she'd been told. There was no controlling the way her cheeks bloomed at the least provocation. And he was right about the grapevine. Ozzie Peyton and Iris Brewer had already dropped some heavy hints and slips. Deliberate ones, she suspected.

"Before you answer, though, there's something I need to do."

"Of course—"

His gaze dropped to her mouth, and her words dried up.

Oh, she thought. He meant he needed to do something right this very minute.

Suddenly she could hardly draw a breath. When his lips touched hers, her mind went absolutely blank for an endlessly long second. Then her senses kicked in, noting the smell of leather, the feel of his oval belt buckle pressing against her stomach, the sound of her own heart beating in her ears.

The sheer size of him surrounded her, made her feel petite and protected. The exquisitely gentle press of his palm on her back made her feel cherished.

She had to remind herself to tread carefully, to act like a lady, to take it slow. Because suddenly she felt wild, had an urgent, pressing need to get hot and sweaty and let desire sweep them over the rapids of sensation.

But Stony was old-fashioned enough to want marriage—even temporarily—rather than an affair. She didn't want to offend.

When she felt the pressure of his body lessen, she found her lips clinging, found herself on tiptoe, trying to hold on to just a split second more of magic. And when she finally had the wherewithal to open her eyes, she knew the expression in them was stunned.

"That answers one of my questions."

She had to clear her throat. "And that was?"

"Chemistry. It's there."

"I'll say."

"And to the other?"

"Huh?" She couldn't seem to think clearly.

"What do you say to the marriage?"

"Oh. Uh, yes."

"Fine. I'll have my attorney get started on the papers, and I'll call the pastor and set something up."

"Um...there's no rush, really. I mean..." That darn heat of embarrassment crept up her neck and burned her ears. "My period's due in the next day or so."

She'd gotten all flustered for nothing. He simply nodded as though speaking of female unmentionables was commonplace. "The weekend then? Friday or Saturday?"

"Saturday should be fine. What will we tell people?"

"What had you planned?"

"I don't know. I guess I hadn't thought explanations would be necessary. That whatever we did behind closed doors would be private."

"Not likely in this town."

"Then I suppose we could say it was love at first sight?"

He shrugged. "That's a stretch, but it'll do."

She felt a swift punch of pain and looked away. They were making a mistake. She'd just agreed to marry this man, and he'd as much as admitted he could never fall in love with her. Granted, she'd only counted on a no-strings, adult relationship but...

What in the world was the matter with her? She didn't *want* him to fall in love with her. She only wanted a baby. Her life was in Texas. There was no excuse to wear her heart on her sleeve. But doggone it...

He hooked a finger under her chin, tipped her face up. "I meant *me*, Eden. You're beautiful. There isn't a man in town who'd question or think twice. The stretch will be in folks believing that beauty fell for the beast. That only happens in fairy tales.''

"Stony—"

He pressed a finger to her lips. There was a resignation in his eyes that made her sad. Words wouldn't work with Stony Stratton. Perhaps that's what he'd gotten from his ex-wife. Eden didn't know. But instinctively she knew that for a man like Stony, a man who watched and studied so deeply, so thoroughly, actions were what he would respond to. Words were just a bunch of letters that made a sound. Actions spoke the truth.

And Eden vowed to make it her mission to show him a very vital truth—that he was a wonderful, sexy, *handsome* man. That exterior wounds were invisible when a man had such a powerfully good and gentle heart.

And that inner goodness made the outer package more handsome and appealing than the hottest movie idol.

She pursed her lips against his finger in a kiss and watched as his whiskey eyes went hot.

She was suddenly aware that they were alone in the house and had just made plans to marry and have an incredibly active sex life.

And after that kiss she was more than anxious to step up the pace a bit. Could she wait a week? My Lord, the changes in her life were coming at such a speed it left her spinning.

WHEN STONY WENT BACK outside to work with his horses, Eden got out bowls, measuring spoons and the canister of flour. Each time she passed by the kitchen window, her heart bumped in her chest.

Lord, he was something. All male. All cowboy. He sat atop a beautiful bay horse, man and animal appearing as one.

And he didn't look a bit like a guy who'd just negotiated marriage with a relative stranger—a stranger who'd propositioned him like a lunatic right here in his very own kitchen.

She scooped shortening into the flour and had it blended before she realized she'd forgotten the salt.

Another sharp cramp tightened her abdomen, and she nearly bent double. Sweat broke out on her neck and hands, making her fingers slick on the slotted spoon.

She was doing the right thing, she told herself.

And as such, she needed to make a call. Picking up the phone, she punched in her long-distance calling card digits, followed by the number for Garden of Eden Catering.

Carrie Mugsannie wasn't just her business partner; she'd been her best friend since kindergarten.

"Garden of Eden, Carrie speaking."

"It's me."

"Eden! I've been a nervous wreck waiting for you to check in with me. So, what's the deal?"

"I'm getting married."

"What?" Carrie shrieked. "Have you lost your mind?"

"Mmm, I haven't truly ruled out the possibility."

"Don't joke…." Carrie paused. "You are joking, right?"

"About losing my mind or the marriage thing?"

"Dang it, Eden. Take your pick."

"He suggested marriage, and I agreed."

For several moments there was silence on the line.

"He's *that* good?"

Eden grinned and added yeast and warm water to her bread mixture. "I don't know yet."

"You don't…Eden, it's only because you're my friend that I didn't lock you in the pantry when you first hatched this whole crazy idea. But marriage? You were only supposed to go there for sex."

"The rules changed."

"The— Okay, I'm sitting down, now. Let's have the whole scoop. Include all the details, please," Carrie requested in an oh-so-prim-and-polite Texas drawl.

Eden laughed, and then she told her friend everything, trying her best to describe Stony, his gentleness, his morals and ethics. "He has to think about his daughter, Carrie. And I agree with him."

"You knew he had a kid when you hightailed it out of here."

"I wasn't thinking."

"Seems to me you're still not."

"Carrie—"

"I know, I know." Carrie's voice softened. "But I have to play the devil's advocate. It's my duty as your friend."

"And I love you for it."

"Okay, so you marry for six months and hope you get pregnant. What if you do and he sues you for custody of the baby?"

"Can't," Eden said. "That's what the legal document is for. And it'll have clauses to protect our business," she assured her friend.

"I'm not concerned about that," Carrie said. "I know you wouldn't jeopardize the company."

Eden refrained from telling her partner that she hadn't had the presence of mind to remember the details, that it had been Stony's suggestion. Granted, she'd have caught it before the actual papers were finalized, but still…

"Legal papers are well and good, but isn't Montana one of those macho states? What if the case went to court and the judge sided with him?"

"You forget who my mother is, Carrie."

"In Texas. That doesn't give her judgeship jurisdiction—or whatever you call it—in Montana. And you said he has custody of his daughter. Did his ex just give it over or was there a battle?"

"I don't know."

"Eden, you should find out these things."

"Maybe his ex didn't *want* Nikki."

"Maybe the cowboy wouldn't let her *have* Nikki," Carrie countered.

Eden didn't want to entertain these doubts. She was getting closer to her goal, taking steps to ensure her dream.

A huge step, she realized.

Or a blind leap, an inner voice taunted.

"I'll find out. And I'm only assuming he's divorced. He might be a widower. He has a scar…" She broke off, feeling she was betraying him somehow by discussing the feature he was most self-conscious of. "Maybe his wife died or something."

"Yeah, and maybe she gave him that scar in a wild and horrible fight—"

"Oh, stop it." Despite the subject matter, Eden

laughed. ''You should hang up your apron and become a writer.''

''Not a chance. Are you sure I can't talk you out of this?''

''You know why I'm doing it, Carrie.''

''Dang it all.'' Carrie sighed, and her voice softened. ''When's the ceremony?''

''Friday or Saturday. I'm not sure. It depends on the lawyer, I think. And the, uh…length of my period.''

''Oh, Eden. Do you want me to fly out?''

''No.'' Eden glanced at the calendar hanging on the wall by the phone. ''We've got the Rammy party scheduled.'' It was a big one, 250 guests for an elaborate buffet, complete with ice sculptures and artistically carved fruits and vegetables. ''Besides, I imagine Stony and I will just go on down to the courthouse.''

She was sure that sounded awful. Carrie's exact sentiments were conveyed in the several moments of silence that followed.

''What about your folks?'' she finally asked. ''You have to tell them.''

''I know. I just wanted to wait, to see if things would work out here.''

''Seems they're working out a little too nicely. You *are* coming back, aren't you?''

''You know I am, Carrie. But, I need…''

''I know. Stupid of me to say anything.''

Eden closed her eyes, took a breath. ''No matter what her age is, a girl just doesn't tell her mom she's off finding some man to sleep with.''

''No,'' Carrie drawled in her best Southern irony tone. ''She discusses it with her mother's best friend. Or should I say *plots* it. What the heck is the difference?''

Eden shrugged. ''Aunt Lottie just always seemed so much more...cool, I guess. Besides, you know my mom. She won't agree with my decision to put off surgery.''

''I'm not so sure I do, either. I've seen you these last few months, Eden, and you scare the daylights out of me.''

''I want a baby, Mugs,'' Eden said softly, tears stinging her eyes before she could stop them.

''Oh, Will, I know.'' Carrie returned, her voice catching. As kids growing up, they'd shortened each other's last names while playing detective—Mugs for Mugsannie, and Will for Williams. And while they were at it, they'd named their future children—Eden's would be Julia or James, and Carrie's would be Crystal or Stephen.

Carrie had gotten both her little Stephen and her little Crystal. And a fabulous husband who adored her.

''I'm just so scared over your health,'' Carrie said.

''I'll be fine.''

''You can adopt, you know. You don't have to go through this.''

''I haven't ruled that out, Mugs. But I have to try this way first.'' Eden wiped dough off her hands and leaned a shoulder against the wall by the phone. She'd been through every stage of Carrie's pregnancy with the twins, up to and including the delivery room. She'd watched every day as Carrie had nurtured those babies in her womb and then had witnessed the absolutely profound miracle of birth.

Sharing the experience had created a need in Eden that was etched on her soul.

"Okay, I'm with you, pal," Carrie said. "If you change your mind, I can be out there quick as a hiccup."

"Thanks. You just take care of the Rammys. I'll call you soon."

When Eden hung up, she covered her bread dough with a towel and set it aside to rise. She told herself it was just as well that Carrie wasn't coming out here for the ceremony. Although they'd vowed to be maid of honor at each other's weddings, this wasn't a true one. It didn't really count.

That thought zinged her like touching bare fingers to a hot cookie sheet.

Still, whether it counted or not, Carrie had raised some questions in Eden's mind, and she knew they would eat at her until she found out.

She washed her hands, took off her apron and went to find Stony, having to traipse through three outbuildings before she nearly ran into him coming out of a round training pen. A beautiful, light bay horse followed docilely, its nose practically pressed to Stony's shoulder.

Astonished, Eden came to a stop. It was the darnedest thing; like a dog adoringly following his owner. The horse didn't have on any headgear—no bridle, reins...nothing. Yet it strolled along behind him, ears twitching happily.

She grinned and pointed out, "You seem to have picked up a shadow."

He stopped in front of her, and the horse stopped, as well, lightly blowing through his nose and nodding his head as though wary, but enough of a gentleman to offer a greeting.

"Meet King Henry VIII."

"Henry VIII?" she repeated.

"Mmm. Registered quarter horse gelding."

She cringed. "I doubt the original king—studly as he thought he was—would appreciate his namesake having his privates clipped."

"Who's gonna tell him?"

Eden grinned and rubbed the horse's cheek. "So what do you call him?"

"Henry. He didn't seem to care for the pretentious, kingly title."

"Told you that, huh? Hello, Henry. Aren't you a beauty."

Again the horse nodded, and Eden laughed.

The bay's coat was shot through with copper highlights, making him gleam in the sunlight. The contrast with his inky black main and tail was striking, as was his proud stance, giving him a regal look worthy of royalty.

Eden stepped back so Stony could continue on toward the stable. Henry politely followed, as did Eden. When they'd reached the bay's stall, Stony asked, "Did you need something?"

"A question answered."

He glanced at her, picked up a currycomb and began combing Henry's coat. "Shoot."

"What was your wife's name?"

A pause. A beat of silence. Then the comb started moving again. "Paula."

"Why did she give up custody of Nikki?"

"That's two questions."

"Is that a crime for somebody who's fixin' to stand in front of a judge with you?"

"Preacher," he corrected.

"We'll discuss that." What they intended surely ought not to take place in the Lord's house. It didn't seem right. "So, why did she?"

"Custody wasn't hers to give up or keep. Nikki was my goddaughter—had been since before I got married. When Nikki's parents died, I immediately started adoption procedures, a promise I'd made and never thought I'd have to keep. Paula wasn't happy about it, wanted me to choose between them." His palm slid down Henry's sleek neck. "I chose Nikki."

"Oh." She hadn't expected that. "Well...um, thank you, then." Flustered, she backed out of Henry's stall and headed toward the sunshine at the open end of the stables, knowing Stony was frowning in consternation at her abrupt exit. For some reason, though, she couldn't seem to find her Southern manners, manners that dictated one must *always* excuse one's self.

With each deliberate step she took, Carrie's warnings tried to take hold, grabbing a little harder, shaking her confidence.

It had been stupid—and subconscious, she realized now—but she'd somehow thought that since Stony had his own child, he wouldn't give her a bad time about keeping hers. Kind of like "one for you and one for me," she supposed, feeling incredibly ashamed that her subconscious mind could even entertain such a notion.

There was absolutely no sense or logic to her

thinking. A testament to her impulsiveness—or shock, perhaps.

She could still recall the doctor's words—or word, rather. The only one she'd really heard past the buzzing in her ears. *Hysterectomy.*

Aunt Lottie's phone call had caught Eden at a low point, a point beyond tears, a point where exhaustion had sent her body and mind into a state of shutdown.

So when her aunt had called back several days later, Eden had grasped the wild suggestion like a drowning victim reaching for the final lifeboat, even if it had holes in it.

She'd blocked out logic.

Embarrassingly so.

Would a man who had the honor, love and loyalty to uphold a vow, to adopt his goddaughter and love her like his own, be a man willing to give up a baby from his own seed?

If there was a baby.

She was placing her faith solely in Stony's goodness, his gentle heart, the man her aunt had described as safe and genuine, the man who had sounded almost too good to be true.

And she hoped to Heaven she wasn't making the biggest mistake of her life.

Chapter Six

Eden knew Stony had already told Nikki about the marriage plans, and as carefree as you please, she'd merely said okay and skipped away. No questions asked. Stony had said he wasn't really surprised at her unconditional acceptance. That's the kind of child she was.

But Eden needed more reassurance.

In Nikki's room, with its fluffy eyelet comforter mussed from being bounced on, and stuffed animals and horse statues strewn about, Eden flicked through the hangers in the little girl's closet, attempting to choose an outfit for the dinner at Brewer's Saloon they were due to attend in a while.

"Dress or pants?" she asked, noting that there weren't a whole lot of dresses to begin with.

"Blue jeans." Nikki giggled and tossed a stuffed animal in the air. It bounced off the ceiling, went off course, and Nikki nearly fell off the bed fielding it on its descent. "Dresses are for church, silly."

Eden gave an exaggerated gasp. "Why, nobody told me that. Suppose folks'll think I'm struttin' my okra if I wear something girly?"

Nikki giggled again, as Eden had intended.

"Nope, 'cuz you're bigger. Uncle Ethan said boys like girls in dresses." Up went the stuffed animal again. This time it didn't go wild, and she caught it in her skinny arms. "But I want my blue jeans. And I like the Barbie shirt. I got pink boots to go with it."

"Well, then. Color coordinated. Excellent fashion sense. You'll be the belle of the ball."

"How come you're marrying my daddy?"

Eden paused, taken off guard by the subject change. She took the pink shirt out of the closet and went to sit on the bed. Nikki hadn't been interested in discussing the subject with Stony. Evidently, she didn't feel the same way with regard to Eden.

And Eden was glad. She needed, desperately, to find out this child's true feelings.

"We thought it would be smart because I'm living in the house with you and your daddy, and... well, it's not the proper thing for a single girl to do. It might look bad to folks."

"But Daddy didn't get married to Lottie."

"She was already married to Ray."

Nikki nodded and bounced up on her knees. "And you're not, so you gotta get married so you can kiss and stuff."

Out of the mouths of babes. In a single sentence the five-year-old had summed up the situation without batting an eye. "Uh, something like that."

"Okay. Can I be a flower girl? I getted to do it two times already, with Hannah and Dora, and I'm real good at it."

Eden smiled, not sure if she was relieved or annoyed at not having to go into a detailed explanation. This was the unworried, accepting attitude Stony had told her about.

"Of course you can dress up and carry flowers. But this will be a little different. I imagine we'll be at the courthouse rather than the church."

"But there's no aisle there." Apparently this was cause for concern. Nikki looked scandalized, nearly pulling the ears off the stuffed rabbit she'd been about to send flying again.

"We can set up some chairs so there will be."

Nikki's features relaxed, and so did her hold on the poor rabbit's ears. "Are you gonna be my mommy then?"

Eden felt a swift squeeze in her heart. This was so delicate. The last thing in the world she wanted to do was hurt this darling child. She wished she'd pinned Stony down about Nikki's parents, what had happened to them that had caused Stony to uphold his vow as the little girl's godfather and adopt her. If she had some idea of Nikki's mother, if Nikki remembered her...

"You have a mommy," she said carefully.

"Yes, but she's an angel now. And she watches me from Heaven. I have a picture. Do you want to see?"

Before Eden could respond, Nikki scrambled across the bed, grabbed a gold-framed photograph off her bedside table and bounced back.

"See?"

"She's beautiful." And so young. As was the man with her in the photo, his laughing face turned toward the camera, his arms around the woman who was obviously the love of his life. Eden had noticed the picture, but had been too distracted to ask about it.

Nikki had suffered a loss, even if she was too young to remember, and Eden didn't want to add another to this child's life.

She would not, could not, go through with her plans at the expense of this child. She had to know how Nikki felt.

"You know, if I had to leave someday, it wouldn't be because I didn't love you all to pieces."

"I know. Daddy says I'm so cute everybody loves me to bits."

The way she said it was so matter-of-fact. Not bratty or prissy or conceited. Just very sure of herself and her place in Stony's household. In his life.

"Where would you hafta go?"

"I have a house in Texas and a job where I cook all kinds of food for people's parties and a very good friend who has two little children close to your age. Their names are Stephen and Crystal. Someday I would have to go home to them."

Lord, how did you tell a child that you were planning the divorce before you'd even taken the walk down the aisle? And did Nikki even understand about divorce? Had she been old enough to feel the turmoil when Stony had gone through it?

"Stephen and Crystal would be sad if you didn't come home?" Nikki asked, her little face a study in compassion.

"I think they would."

"Do you have a mommy?"

"Yes. She's a judge."

"Like old Judge Lester in town? He wears black

jammies to work. Does your mom wear her jammies to work?''

Eden grinned. ''A robe, yes. Fun job, huh?''

''I think I'll be a judge when I grow up.''

''It's a very noble profession.''

''Is your daddy a judge?''

''No. He's a chef at his own restaurant.''

Nikki giggled. ''He cooks?''

''Yes. And very well, at that.''

''That's how come you cook, huh?''

''Probably.''

''Okay.''

''Okay, what?'' Eden asked.

''It's okay if you have to go back home sometime. But I can't come, too, 'cuz I gotta stay here with Daddy or he would be sad.''

''Of course you do.'' Eden swallowed hard. At times this little girl seemed far beyond her five years. Well adjusted, happy and secure. Because of Stony. ''So we'll be very good friends, you and I?''

''The best.''

''Then what do you say we take this outfit and run on down to my room. We'll be girls and primp together.''

Nikki was off the bed in a flash, the abandoned rabbit landing with a thump on the pine floor beside the headboard.

WHEN STONY CAME DOWNSTAIRS, several aromas hit him at once. Warm, yeasty bread, lemon furniture polish—and the scent of a woman fresh from a bath.

The latter gave him a couple of touch-and-go moments where his body screamed for mastery over his mind.

Since their marriage agreement yesterday, and Eden's question about Paula, they'd pretty much been avoiding each other. He gave a mental shrug. In truth there wasn't any reason to hang around together until it was time…

He didn't even want to get hung up on that line of thinking. It was difficult enough as it was to keep his mind on the horses and off the soul-stirring images of Eden in bed. With him. By this coming weekend.

And the smell of steamy wildflowers emanating from her room off the kitchen wasn't helping one bit.

In fifteen years he couldn't remember ever noticing Lottie or Ray's bath perfumes. He was sure he'd never come into the kitchen and been surrounded by moist air shimmering with feminine scent, the kind of scent that made a man's mouth water and his hormones jump to attention.

He focused on the loaves of bread, muffins and little dessert things all decorated and wrapped in cellophane that lined the countertops. Eden had been busy.

He took a closer look at the fancy sweets. Some looked like cookies and others like miniature cakes or tarts.

She didn't just bake a cake or pie like most. She fixed a whole bunch of different stuff. He hadn't known he had such a variety of ingredients in his pantry. Maybe he should just taste one, he thought.

"Daddy! Kiss my lips!"

His hand jerked back to his side, and he turned

as Nikki came streaking out of Eden's room, her
cherry lips a little rosier and glossier than normal.

Nikki leaped the last step, and he caught her up
in his arms, dutifully pecking her pursed lips.

"It's strawberry, do you taste it?"

He licked his lips. "Mmm, hmm."

"Eden put it on me. And she gots it on her lips,
too. 'Cept hers is banana." Nikki pressed her lips
together, rubbing the gloss and having another lick.
"You could taste that one, too, if you want."

His gaze slowly shifted to Eden. She stood in the
doorway wearing a cap-sleeved silver dress in some
soft-looking material that made him want to reach
out and touch. The dress was plain and simple,
clinging to her breasts without appearing to and
flowing in a silky slide down her body like white-
hot liquid mercury, the midthigh length emphasizing
legs that were tanned and toned and seemed to go
on forever. The black, pointed-toe boots with silver
tooling were well broken in, as was the black, wide-
brimmed Stetson with a cattleman's crease and a
braided silver band that she clutched in her hand.

He felt a smile tug at his mouth when she pressed
her lips together, much the same as Nikki had done.
But where Nikki's thoughts were purely innocent,
Eden's were obviously on a different page. It
showed in the bloom of color on her cheeks, cheeks
that were looking paler than normal, he noted.

And as much as he wanted to taste her lips, with
or without the banana, he didn't dare.

"I'm full from tasting your strawberries," he told
Nikki, noting that she also wore a powdery dusting
of subtle color on her eyelids and cheeks. "Besides,
you ladies don't want to go around letting every man

in the county taste your glossy stuff. It'll get all smeared.'' He set Nikki down and shoved his hands in his pockets.

"How come we're havin' the Fourth of July dinner when we already did the sparklers?'' Nikki asked.

"I already told you, doll baby,'' Eden said, moving out of the doorway and squeezing Nikki's sweet cheeks as she passed. ''Today is the actual holiday. We just celebrated it on the weekend, because that's when most folks have their parties.''

Stony looked back at the abundance of food on the counters. "This isn't a potluck. I'm buying tonight.''

"I know—I mean not that you're buying…I have my own money. But I got carried away again.'' She loaded bread and muffins into cardboard boxes. ''I thought I'd share with the neighbors.''

"I imagine they'll appreciate it.'' He caught the first box she shoved at him. ''And I'm still buying.'' To prevent an argument, he snagged a second carton and went out to the truck. Intending to go back for the rest, he turned and nearly stepped on his tongue.

Eden was already coming out the door toward him, her Stetson on her head, a box in her arms, a huge purse slung over her shoulder and that flirty, short dress swaying as she walked, teasing her thighs with a silky bounce that damn near bewitched him.

Dragging his gaze up, he reached out and took the box from her. "I'd have come back for it.''

"And I saved you some steps.''

"I don't mind a few steps," he muttered, his voice more gruff than usual.

"Ah, chivalry. A lost art. And I *do* like that in a man."

Her Texas drawl and sassy green eyes beguiled him. If he'd been walking, he would have tripped. He took a deep, calming breath, put the box in the back seat of the extended-cab truck and lifted Nikki in, helping her with her seat belt.

He started to step back to give Eden room to maneuver, when she suddenly laughed, the sound arresting him right where he stood.

"Did I miss something?" he asked, brows raised.

"Not yet. And you won't, either, if you keep standing there." When he still just stared at her, not having the slightest idea what she was talking about, she laughed again. "I'm trying to figure out how to gracefully climb up in this truck with a minimum of panty flash."

Panty... His gaze whipped to the hem of her short dress. Flashing her underpants, she meant.

Bewitching *and* charming.

"Allow me to practice a little more chivalry." He slipped the heavy purse from her shoulder and spanned her waist with his hands. "You're in charge of keeping your legs together," he said casually as he lifted her onto the leather seat. Cautioning himself not to linger, when he wanted to do so in the worst way, he bent to retrieve her purse and set it in her lap.

Her green eyes were wide and a little stunned, kind of like a mustang staring down at his rider on the ground, wondering how in the heck he'd gotten there.

He patted her knee. "There. Not even a flash of green underwear."

"They're black," she exclaimed before she realized he was teasing her. Her expression turned to surprise, then to laughter.

He was a little surprised himself that he was teasing—flirting, actually. It had been a long time. It felt good.

WHEN THEY REACHED Brewer's Saloon, Stony elected to leave the food in the truck. He'd bring Wyatt and Ethan out to help with the transfer. Besides, he imagined he was going to need a break, a cool brace of fresh air if he had to watch Eden move in that incredible dress all evening and smell the warm, enticing wildflower scent of her skin.

When they stepped through the door, Eden put her hand on Stony's arm. "Excuse me for a moment. I need to use the ladies' room."

He nodded, pointed out the direction, then went to find their seats. The booths, with red-and-white-checked tablecloths, were filling up. He stepped through the swinging saloon doors, where a couple of pool tables edged a wooden dance floor. He saw that his neighbors had already pushed together a bunch of tables. Brewer's longtime waitress, Maedean, expertly wove through the crowd with a tray of drinks held high.

"Hey, there, Stony. What'll it be?"

He didn't want to be presumptuous by ordering for Eden, yet at the same time, he wanted to save Maedean some steps. He'd noticed that she drank a lot of fruit juices and figured that would be a safe enough choice. "Beer, orange juice and a Shirley

Temple.'' If Eden decided she wanted a kicker in that juice it'd be easy enough to get.

"All together?" Maedean teased.

"Separate might be nice," he said dryly.

Maedean laughed.

"Lots of cherries," Nikki shouted, and took off to the other side of the room to show off her makeup and help Ian push buttons on the jukebox.

"You got it, darlin'." Maedean disappeared through the swinging doors toward the bar, and Stony went over to check out the hot-and-heavy pool game taking place between Dora Callahan and Wyatt Malone.

Wearing her signature tight jeans and cute little tank top, Dora was leaning across the pool table, lining up her shot, her wheat-blond hair falling across her shoulder, getting in her face. Hannah Malone, supporting her swollen stomach with her hands, gave Dora encouragement as Ethan and the preacher seemed to feel honor bound to stick up for the guy team.

"These girls are whippin' our butts," Ethan said, reaching out a hand to shake Stony's. "Where's your date?"

"Ladies' room. And she's not my date."

"Hell, Stratton. I wouldn't be saying that too loud, seeing as you're getting married to her in a few days' time."

Dora raised up from her shot and put an arm around Stony's neck in a quick hug. "Ethan, hush, you weren't going to say anything," she admonished her husband.

"I'm not the one with the flapping lips."

Stony shifted his gaze and scowled at the

preacher, who lifted his shoulders and tried not to make direct eye contact.

"Thanks a lot, Dan."

"Sorry," the pastor said. "It slipped out. Ozzie's fault."

Man alive, he hadn't seen the town passing the buck like this in a long time—and headed by the preacher, no less. Then again, Dan Lucas hadn't always been an ordained minister. They'd grown up together, and Stony remembered when Dan had landed in Judge Lester's court for taking old man Grisby's tractor—without permission—and driving it straight down the center of Main Street.

Drunk as a polecat.

And now, here he was, young and cocky...and responsible for praying over their souls.

Stony shook his head and noticed the four matchmakers at their regular table in a corner that lately had been cordoned off and declared the cigar-smoking section. But only when the kids weren't present. Iris Brewer was a tiny woman, but it was clear who ran the show around here.

Ozzie Peyton shifted forward in his chair, pinning Stony with a disapproving look. Stony had no idea what he'd done to deserve the look, was sure he *didn't* deserve it. Then Ozzie's expression cleared, and he eased back in his chair.

The reason, Stony realized, had just come through the swinging saloon doors, her black Stetson tipped low and sexy over her forehead. Red hair cascaded down her back and shoulders, catching the overhead light and shimmering like fire against the silvery sheen of her dress.

With boots that seemed to glide across the room,

she automatically picked up the rhythm of the Brooks and Dunn tune and moved in a smooth two-step walk across the floor.

Every man in the room watched her, and Stony felt a queer kick right under his ribs. One word, one look from those expressive green eyes, and she'd have more applicants willing to help her out than she could handle.

So why the hell had she picked him?

For that matter, why hadn't Lottie recommended someone else?

And thinking about one of these other cowboys touching Eden made him crazy.

"Hey there, Tex," Ethan said. Perched on his arm was his baby daughter, Katie. On his face was a wide grin aimed at Eden, but clearly meant to annoy Stony.

"Can't you come up with more original stuff, Callahan?" Stony knew his tone was abrupt, and there was no call for it. Ethan's flirting was harmless. Blatantly so. Anybody with a speck of vision could see he was crazy in love with his wife—a dedicated family man and proud of it.

"Are you speaking to my clothes or my home state?" Eden asked with an open smile that suggested she had this man's measure and that they could very likely become the best of friends.

"The state," Stony answered for his friend. "He forgets he's a married man and not a Casanova any longer."

"Casanova is the name of Wyatt's bull," Ethan said, unfazed. "And your clothes are mighty fine, too, Ms Eden," he added, cutting his twinkling gaze to Stony.

Stony sighed, surprised he felt the punch of annoyance…and jealousy. Ethan was his friend, for crying out loud. He was holding his baby girl in his arms. And Dora was standing right there in earshot, laughing and poking her husband in the ribs.

Iris Brewer bustled into the room carrying a tray stacked high with burgers and hot dogs. "You boys take off your hats."

Every man in the room whipped off their hat and raked a hand through their hair—and so did Eden.

"Where are my manners?" Eden asked, grinning, her soft Southern drawl sliding over Stony like an erotic touch.

"Not you, love," Iris said. "Your hat is part of your outfit."

"Mine's part of the whole package, too," Stony pointed out.

"And a very nice package, indeed. But you'll be polite during dinner. You can put it back on when the dancing starts. Nothing sexier looking than a cowboy gliding his lady across the dance floor with his head bent and his hat tipped low."

Iris busily arranged food and the old fellas grumbled about bossy women. She shot them a quelling look and encouraged everyone to sit and eat.

Now that Eden's hat wasn't shading her face, Stony noticed the pallor of her skin.

"You okay?"

"Of course." She smiled at him—forced, he realized. To anyone else in the room it would have looked genuine. But Stony saw more than most. Eyes often spoke, and if you looked closely enough, listened, you could see beneath the surface.

Looking at her, he saw beauty and milky-white

skin framed by hair the color of a blood bay, shot through with deep, wine-red highlights. Dimples gave her smile a mischievous air, an openness that clearly showed she was a woman who loved people, interacted easily with them, a woman who genuinely had fun wherever she went. The unselfconscious way she'd picked up the rhythm of the music, moving her body to it as she'd made her way across the room a few minutes ago, said it for her.

But in her eyes was weariness. And fear, he realized, his brows pulling together.

He slipped the big tote-style purse off her shoulder and pulled out a chair for her to sit on.

She smiled and her dimples flashed. "A girl could get spoiled by you."

"You bet," Ozzie Peyton said, coming up behind them. "A gentleman's what his grandma raised him to be. Good teachin', you bet. Don't you just love to hear this gal talk?" Ozzie asked with a glance at Stony.

Stony was still imagining ways to spoil Eden Williams. When she looked up at him, he held her gaze, steadily, deliberately.

Regardless of his looks, there was one area he was totally confident about: he knew how to please a woman. "Yeah. I like the accent."

"Well, then," Ozzie said, a bit nervously. That little bit of eyeball communication was a scorcher and meant to be private. He nearly rubbed his hands together in glee. "I'll just step right out of the fire here and take a seat." Vivid blue eyes twinkled as he scurried away, obviously to report back to his cronies.

Eden cleared her throat. "They're matchmaking, you know."

"I figured that out." He sat down beside her.

"I'm sorry."

He glanced at her, frowned. "For what?"

"For dragging this out so publicly." She raked her teeth over her bottom lip. "Aunt Lottie told me you were a private man, and I'd hoped to give you the option of keeping what went on between us private."

"You think I'm embarrassed that folks know we're…together?"

"I hope not." She flicked her hair behind her ear. "I just wanted—"

"I don't mind, Eden."

She nodded. Then a look of distress passed over her pale features. She smiled, put a hand on his thigh and gave a squeeze, nearly sending him straight up out of the chair.

"Excuse me a moment, will you?" She picked up her oversize purse, slung it over her shoulder like a backpack and headed in the direction of the rest rooms.

It was a trek she made just about every half hour over the course of the evening. And each time she returned, her smile was a little brighter, her skin a little paler. He made a point of noting the time, watching her closely.

Something wasn't right, yet each time he started to ask, she would shake her head, smile at him and continue visiting with the neighbors, laughing and joking—and unobtrusively excusing herself to go to the ladies' room.

By nine o'clock, Stony had had enough.

He headed over to where she sat chatting with Vera Tillis.

Everyone at the table looked at him expectantly as he stopped by Eden's chair, gazed down at her. Holding out his hand, palm up, he said, "Dance with me."

It wasn't a question, and he didn't give her an opportunity to answer, much less choose not to. He carefully pulled her to her feet and drew her onto the dance floor.

The feel of the soft dress under his palm nearly sidetracked him. A kind of velvet, he noted, yet not really velvet. With his palm low on her back, he could feel the elastic waistband of her panties. Or maybe a slip, he wasn't sure.

Wyatt was dancing with Hannah, her pregnant belly like a basketball between them. Ethan danced by with Dora, and from the way he was looking at his wife, somebody was surely going to suggest he either get a room or take her home.

Couples, Stony thought.

He hadn't imagined he'd ever be one again.

"I like your neighbors, Stony."

"So do I. Now do you want to tell me what's going on with you?" Tiny blue veins mapped the inside of her arms, the back of her hands, the slow pulse at her temple. Lines of pain pulled at the corners of her eyes. It almost hurt him to see it. "You're sick, aren't you?"

She shook her head, rested her cheek against his shoulder.

"Did I ever tell you about my grandmother?" He didn't wait for an answer. "She was deaf—born that way. She could speak, but rarely chose to do so. So the majority of our communication was in sign language. I learned to listen when hands spoke, to notice nuances, changes in mood, for instance, sadness…physical pain.''

She sighed and whispered something he couldn't hear over the music.

''What?'' He bent down so they were cheek to cheek.

''I started my period,'' she repeated, embarrassment tingeing her voice.

He stopped dancing, cupped her chin and tipped her face up so he could get a good look at her. A strong wind would knock her down. He felt his heart kick behind his ribs. ''Is that why you've gone to the bathroom every half hour?''

A hint of color stained her ashy cheeks. She nodded. ''Don't worry. It's usually only like this for a couple of days.''

A couple of days? He knew the workings of a woman's body—no subject had been taboo with his grandmother, plus he'd also been married for two years. So he had a fairly good grasp of what was happening here.

At the rate Eden was going, she might not *survive* a couple of days.

Chapter Seven

After Stony got Nikki settled in bed, he made his way back downstairs. The light from the bathroom spilled a yellow glow over Lottie and Ray's bedroom, outlining Eden's body curled in a ball on the bed.

"How often do you go through this?"

Eden hugged her stomach and swallowed back the wimpy emotions that sneaked past her defenses around this time every month, making her impatient because she had little control. The pain made her nauseous. That Stony was witnessing it embarrassed her to no end.

"I'm fine." She waved him away. "I'll be better in the morning." Not likely.

He sighed. "You're not fine. Tell me what to do to help you."

"Leave."

He shook his head, carefully sat down on the bed beside her. "That's not one of the options. Did you take anything for the pain?"

"No. It'll be okay." Getting up would simply be too much. If she could just be still for a few minutes she'd manage. It would pass.

He was quiet for a long time before she felt the mattress shift, realized he was leaving, respecting her wishes. She told herself she was relieved, that the lump in her throat was the product of pain. Besides, she'd just as soon be alone with her misery. She had never liked people witnessing a weakness in her. She was always the one who led the way, the one who got out of bed no matter what, who'd baked five hundred lemon tarts with a blinding, raging headache.

A headache she was now experiencing with a vengeance.

The backs of Stony's knuckles lightly brushing her cheek made her jump like a scalded cat.

"Easy." He sat back down on the side of the bed, slid an arm under her shoulders and lifted her.

Eden barely suppressed a moan. Anything straighter than a curled position felt like torture.

"Take these."

She saw that he held two of her prescription pain pills.

"I don't usually go through a lady's purse, but it occurred to me on my way to get aspirins that a doctor would probably have prescribed something much stronger for you."

"Thank you." She put the pills in her mouth and sipped the water he held to her lips. "I'm sorry to be such a bother."

"Hush now."

His kindness simply undid her. Tears leaked from the corners of her eyes, not just from the excruciating cramps wrenching her body, but from the deeper pain, the knowledge that what she was experiencing right now was the ticking time bomb that could cause her to lose a very vital and important part of her womanhood.

"Oh, man," Stony said. "Don't do that. Shhh." He hooked his hand under her knees and brought her onto his lap, holding her as she curled into his chest.

"The curse of women," she whispered. "We just get so weepy, and the next thing you know, we're squalling for no good reason."

Hardly jiggling her, he scooted back against the headboard, stroked her hair, her arms, the sides of her legs. "I'd say you've got plenty of reason."

His chest was so broad, his shoulders and arms thick with muscles, his palms wide and oh, so gentle as they passed up and down over the silk of her pajamas. He surrounded her. Made her feel cherished.

He was the kind of man most women only dreamed of.

The kind of man she could easily fall in love with.

She groaned again, and his arms tightened, holding her more securely, pulling her knees tighter toward her chest.

"Shhh." His cheek rested against the top of her head, his breath stirring the hair at her temple. "Relax. The medication'll kick in soon."

And although it did succeed in easing the pain, sleep wasn't one of the perks. Not with the way she had to get up and down all night.

Stony was afraid to leave her side, and by morning he was a wreck.

That's why he'd called and dragged the doctor out of bed at the crack of dawn.

"Thanks for coming, Chance." He shook the

doctor's hand and filled him in on the nature of the problem and his concerns.

When they went into Eden's room, she was just coming out of the bathroom. Again.

She uttered a feminine sound of distress.

"Well, then. This is a fine how d'you do, and I don't believe it's covered in the etiquette books." Her drawl was even more pronounced, and in a show of modesty, she raised her hand to the lapels of her pajamas. "I'm sure y'all will excuse me. I'm not exactly dressed for entertaining company, and to be honest, I ought to mention that I'm feeling about as friendly as a bramble bush right now."

Stony admired her quick wit, the way she handled any situation she was thrust into. Pale as a ghost, in her pajamas, she was the perfectly contrite and correct Southern hostess. A lady right down to her toes.

Too damn good for the likes of him.

"Eden, this is Dr. Hammond."

Eden finger combed her hair, wishing there was a hole she could hide in right quick. "I appreciate your concern, Stony, but this truly isn't necessary." She looked at the doctor. The very young and handsome doctor. "I'm sorry, Doctor Hammond. Stony's apparently worried that I'm about ready to give up my guitar for a harp, and I can assure you, I'm not."

The doctor laughed, and Stony frowned.

"Call me Chance. And let me be the judge of what's necessary. It's one of my specialties." He held out his arm in a gesture indicating she should hop back in bed.

This might very well be his specialty, Eden thought, but she still didn't like being fussed over. It had been mortifying enough to discuss her female health issues with Stony, to have him practically *witness* the whole thing up close and personal for goodness' sake. And now they expected her to go through explanations all over again? In front of both of them?

"Really, this isn't—"

Stony's hand cupped her shoulder, squeezed gently. "I've explained the nature of your condition to Chance," he said softly, understanding her discomfort and reservations. "For my peace of mind, will you just let him have a look at you?"

When he spoke to her in that incredibly tender voice, how could she refuse him? And there really wasn't any call to be embarrassed about her state of undress. Her satin pajamas were the equivalent of silky pants and a shirt, perfectly modest.

"Just your vitals and some questions," Chance added.

She smiled. "I assure you, I've still got a pulse. And by the way," she said, holding out her hand. "It's very nice to meet you."

"Same goes." He waited until she'd settled back in the bed, then checked her heart and pulse rate, the reaction of her eyes and the color of her fingernails. "Any fainting spells?"

"No."

"Dizziness?"

"Comes with the territory."

"Would you recognize the signs of shock?"

She nodded. "Weakness, shallow breathing, rapid heart beat, clammy skin, confusion." She'd experienced every one of these symptoms in the past few days, and they had nothing to do with shock and everything to do with the soul-stirring, six-and-a-half-foot cowboy who was practically hovering behind the doctor.

"Anemia's nothing to mess around with," Chance said solemnly.

She met his gaze squarely. "I know. I'm taking supplements to compensate."

He picked up the bottles from the nightstand, checked the dosage and nodded. He studied her for a long moment. "Six months might be too long to let this go on."

Her gaze whipped to Stony, and although his expression never changed, she knew he'd told the doctor her goal, the reason they were getting married. Her face burned even as her back straightened and her shoulders squared.

"I'm going to hope and pray like mad that it isn't." She felt the familiar ache in the back of her throat, the sting in her eyes. She hated the emotional upheaval. "I'm not foolish, Dr. Hammond," she said quietly. "I know my body and what it'll handle."

"Then I'll be pulling for you." His eyes were filled with compassion.

"Thank you."

Chance stood and began putting instruments back in his bag. "You're drinking? Keeping yourself hydrated?"

"Good old Gatorade."

He nodded. "Know your blood type?"

"A-positive."

"Mine's O-positive," Stony volunteered, his tone grave. "If the need arose, could I donate?"

"Oh, for Pete's sake," Eden said. "Let's not get

too morbid.'' Never mind that the color of her skin alone suggested she could use a transfusion.

Chance smiled and nodded at Stony. ''O's universal.'' Looking back at Eden, he asked, ''Got everything you need here? I can send one of the women from town if you need supplies.''

''I'm fine.'' Cryin' out loud, even with a pitifully low blood count, her skin still turned pink. She could hold her own in any conversation, anywhere, but talking about feminine supplies and bodily functions in mixed company this way was as awkward as in-laws on a honeymoon.

While Stony walked the doctor out, Eden slipped into the bathroom and got dressed. Her reflection in the mirror was enough to scare the quills off a porcupine. Her hair looked even redder against the colorless hue of her skin, and her eyes…well, that was a sorry sight. She looked as though she'd gone three rounds with Mohammed Ali's daughter and definitely come up the loser.

Given her sorry appearance, she wouldn't be surprised if Stony withdrew his proposal.

Doing what she could to disguise her ashy complexion with makeup, Eden quickly plaited her hair in a French braid and gave herself a pep talk. ''There's always a blessing, Eden. Be thankful you're one of the lucky ones whose period only lasts a few days.''

Satisfied that she'd gone as far as she could with her pitiful appearance, she opened the bathroom door and ran smack dab into Stony.

He steadied her with his hands at her elbows. His brows drew together, pulling at the scar on his face. ''What are you doing?''

"Getting dressed." She smiled at him, touched by his concern, his solicitousness. "Did you think I'd had a spell and fallen out the bathroom?"

"You look like a feather would knock you over."

"You're being very kind," she said on a laugh. "I just got a good gander at myself in the mirror."

The intensity of his amber gaze made her breath stop for half a heartbeat.

"You're beautiful even when you're sick." His tone was soft, reluctant even, as though the compliment made him vulnerable somehow.

"I'm not sick."

His brows rose. She loved the way he spoke without even using his mouth or vocal cords. It did, however, unsettle her a bit, sent her nerves scrambling.

She cleared her throat. "What I am, though, is starving. So, if you'll step aside, I'll get in there and fix us up a feast."

"No, you won't."

"Excuse me?" It had been many a year since someone had told her no in just that tone.

"You go back to bed. I'll cook."

"Don't be ridiculous. Your expertise is the horses. Mine's cooking. I could have one foot planted in the daisies and an arm tied behind my back and still fix a five-course meal."

His lips twitched and a smile lit his eyes. "Is that so?"

"I hope to shout." Standing toe-to-toe with him, she nodded, daring him to try that bossiness again. Give her a stool pulled up to the stove to sit on, put a spatula in her hand, and she could go to town.

"I wondered about that red hair."

Her breath actually hissed. "Yes, I have a temper,

as cliché as that sounds. It doesn't rear up often, but when it does, it's ugly.''

''I'll keep that in mind. In the meantime there's no shortage of rope around here.''

She frowned, thrilled with the smile that lingered in his eyes, yet wary, nonetheless. ''Meaning?''

''Meaning if need be I can tie you in that bed.''

Laughter burst out from her. She knew she should be upset with his bossiness, but she just couldn't work up any steam. She put her hand on his chest. ''I'm afraid I'm not up to that kind of play just now.''

Where there was amusement in his eyes before, now there was heat.

The heat of sensual promise.

A host of butterflies fluttered in her stomach, winged through her chest, taking her breath. She swayed, realized that desire was making her weak in more ways than just sexual.

''See there?'' He put an arm around her to steady, pulled her to him for just a moment, a moment that didn't last nearly long enough. ''Now don't give me a hard time. You rest today.''

She hadn't even realized he'd walked her backward until her knees hit the side of the mattress. ''Stony, really this isn't—''

''If you say *necessary,* I really am going to get the rope.''

She giggled, surprised at the sound, then dropped her forehead to his chest and surrendered gracefully. ''Then I'll say thank you, and allow you to be my Sir Galahad.''

''Thought so.''

JULY 15. MY WEDDING DAY. The words rolled around and around in Eden's mind, making her palms damp against the small beige purse clutched in her hands.

Instead of jumping right into the ceremony, as originally discussed, they'd ended up waiting an extra week in order to get legal matters taken care of. The added days had given her a chance to build up her strength—it also put her that much closer to the crucial days when her body could possibly conceive.

Now there wouldn't be time for her and Stony to ease into intimacy as she'd hoped, to relax, get comfortable, get it right. Her feminine clock was on its unstoppable path, like the ball dropping in Times Square, counting down the days to fertility. If she missed that cycle, she'd be thirty days farther from her goal…thirty days closer to a health decision that would take part of her womanhood and very likely wrench a piece of her soul.

As Stony pulled the truck into the courthouse parking lot, Eden stared at the redbrick building, thinking of her mother.

They'd spoken yesterday, and as Eden had predicted, Beverley Williams had immediately announced she'd be on the first plane headed for Montana. It had taken all of Eden's excuses to prevent that from happening.

Her mother, normally a levelheaded, fair-minded woman—naturally, since she was a judge—had thrown a hissy fit when Eden had come clean about her plans. After she'd pretty much gotten that out of her system, she'd vacillated between stunned disbelief and a mother's profound worry.

Tears stung Eden's eyes as she remembered the

conversation. "Eden, I beg you not to take this chance with your health."

"I have to, Mama. I've told you what the alternative is, and if it ends up that I do have to have the surgery, the only way I could bear it is by knowing that I gave pregnancy my best shot."

"But marriage, darling?"

"It's a small price to pay for a chance at my dream. He has a young, impressionable daughter. He's a good man, Mama. Aunt Lottie will tell you."

Beverley had gone silent, and Eden knew she was weighing the facts as they'd been presented, digesting them, coming to terms with them. "I should still come out. This is your wedding. Your first."

"No! Mama, please. It's not…real. It's only temporary." That still gave her a punch of guilt, of stomach-trembling reservations. The committee on her left shoulder—the voice of her conscience, which often exasperated her to no end—nagged at her that this was wrong, wrong, wrong, while the committee on her right whispered that she had to try, that the greatness of the need canceled out the wrong and made it a right.

"Besides," she told her mother, "you'd cause absolute chaos in the judicial system if you up and hopped a plane on the spur of the moment. That has to be your first concern."

"No. You're wrong there, my love," Beverley had said softly, *very* softly. "You're more important to me than any case, any job…and much, *much* more important than the prospect of a grandchild."

Eden's forced bravery had crumbled at that point, and she'd wept. It had taken another ten minutes to repair that foolish loss of control and convince her mother it wasn't necessary to fly to Montana.

"We're here," Stony said, jerking her out of her musing. The red blur in front of her eyes once again focused into the shape of the courthouse. An American flag flew atop the building, undulating in the afternoon breeze like the ripple of the finest, softest silk.

Eden took a breath, smiled. "Then I guess it's show time." Getting out of the truck, she helped Nikki down. "Come, my little flower girl. Let's see if the judge set us up an aisle for you to stroll prettily down."

"Okay! Come on, Daddy!" Holding Eden's hand, Nikki reached for Stony's hand with the other. Connecting them. Making them look like family.

Eden glanced at Stony. "Are you sure you want to do this for me?"

With his free hand he reached out as though he would stroke her cheek, then hesitated and instead gave a tug to the brim of his Stetson. "Let's go."

He hadn't answered, and all sorts of anxieties started to build inside Eden.

When she entered through the side door of the courthouse, those anxieties stood up and howled.

Instead of Judge Lester waiting for them, Pastor Lucas rose to his feet, a bible in his hands.

And he wasn't alone. Stony's neighbors and friends were there, too—Wyatt, Hannah and Ian Malone; Ethan, Dora and baby Katie Callahan; Iris and Lloyd Brewer; Vera and Vern Tillis; Henry Jenkins and Ozzie Peyton.

Oh, no. Eden hadn't counted on this. Her gaze whipped to Stony. Had he planned it?

He shook his head, understanding her panic. "Not me." He looked as bewildered as she felt. "I've never known the preacher to tell somebody's business like this."

"But I thought the judge was going to perform the ceremony."

He shrugged. "That was the plan. Then Dan got wind of it and said he was offended that we weren't having him do it, and…heck, I lied through my teeth. Told him he'd gotten the whole story wrong. What can I say? I went to school with the guy. But I didn't invite half the town."

Eden swallowed hard, feeling like a fraud. Stony might have fibbed to the preacher, but Eden felt as though she was lying to the whole town.

Her stomach did a flip-flop and she seriously thought she might be ill.

"Excuse me, please." She tried not to run, tried to see past the blinding white specks before her eyes, coached herself to get through the bathroom door before she came undone.

Ladies didn't cause a stir in public.

And it would surely cause a stir if she told Stony right there in front of God and everybody that she'd changed her mind, that she couldn't go through with the marriage plans, after all. His friends were under the impression they'd fallen in love at first sight. They had no idea this was only a smoke screen to legitimize an affair intended solely for procreation.

She leaned against the bathroom sink, splashed water on her face. The door opened, and she whirled around.

In filed Hannah, Dora, Iris and Vera. An instant before the door swung shut, she caught a glimpse of

Ozzie, Henry, Lloyd and Vern looking as though they were mightily tempted to forego the dictates of polite society and ignore the gender sign on the door.

"There, now, love," Iris fussed. "Are you feeling ill? Faint? Or just a plain-old attack of wedding nerves?"

They were all so wonderful. "I can't do this," Eden whispered.

"Why ever not?" Vera asked.

"Because it's not right. We didn't fall in love at first sight like y'all think we did." Well, perhaps *she* had, but that was her own folly to deal with later. With or without Stony's seed, she would eventually go back to Texas. That's where her life was. It would be hard enough carrying her own bittersweet emotions in her heart. To add the hurt feelings of these genuine people to her conscience would be too much to bear.

They'd extended her their friendship. She owed them the truth.

"I came here to get pregnant. By Stony. That's all." Wanting to redeem herself in some small way, even though none of the four women facing her appeared upset, Eden told them her problem.

Iris was the first to speak when Eden had finished. "We know, dear. It about broke our hearts when Lottie told us."

"All of you?" Eden asked.

Hannah and Dora shook their heads. "Those crafty old geezers are picky who they let into their club," Dora said. "Eventually, though, the word trickled down to us. Nothing stays secret for long around here."

"I hope we haven't embarrassed you," Hannah said.

"No. I…you're all so nice. You don't think I'm a horrible person for doing this?"

Everyone shook their heads.

"Even if the preacher ought to say 'in six months do you part' rather than the traditional vow?"

There was a mixture of expressions—understanding, amusement, compassion.

Vera Tillis stepped forward, took Eden's hands in hers. "Getting you this baby is important, honey. And I imagine there'll be times where your heart will just be crushed." She didn't need to elaborate; those times would be when her monthly cycle drained her energy and dashed her hopes. "Stony Stratton is the best man in the world to lead you through that time."

Yes, he was. Having gotten these women's blessings, Eden took a deep breath, gave a smile that trembled only slightly at the corners.

"I'm really happy that y'all came."

"Of course you are," Iris fussed. "Now let's get you back to your groom before he thinks you've changed your mind and we've decided to have a sleepover in the ladies' room."

AND THAT'S EXACTLY what Stony was wondering—if Eden had changed her mind.

He realized, perhaps even for the first time, that the desire for a baby had to be really important to Eden for her to accept him in the bargain, too.

Even though it was only temporary.

But the longer he stood outside the judge's chambers—with six men all pretending nonchalance and diligently avoiding eye contact—the more he worried that she'd changed her mind.

He told himself it didn't matter.

She didn't really want *him*. She only wanted what he could give her. It would be her loss, not his.

Then he saw her coming out of the bathroom, gliding toward him, her broomstick skirt swirling around her ankles, her glossy lips trembling on the verge of a smile, a silent apology.

And he realized it *had* mattered after all.

Their gazes met, and he saw that there would indeed be a wedding today. He released the breath he'd been holding, not sure if he was relieved or sorry.

It would be awfully easy to read more into the relationship than was there.

And that'd be just plain stupid.

Chapter Eight

Nikki had gone home with Hannah, happy to play with Ian for the next few days, and Eden was suffering an attack of nerves.

They were married. And alone.

Her heart began to pound, and her insides quivered as he pulled the truck into the circular driveway in front of the ranch house and shut off the engine.

Now that she knew for certain they would make love, she couldn't look at him without feeling a range of emotions—giddy one minute, then shy the next, hot, then embarrassed.

Sex should be spontaneous. Yet they were planning it. Or at least she was.

Somewhere during the turmoil of her thoughts, Stony had come around to her side of the truck and opened the door. Gallantry, she thought. A gentleman.

A *gentle man.*

She took his hand and let him help her down. Their bodies brushed, igniting a fire in Eden's belly. He didn't speak, just studied her for what seemed like endless moments, the intensity in his amber eyes unnerving her, making her unable to hold his gaze.

She had no idea what this tall, incredibly virile cowboy was thinking when he looked at her.

She didn't know how to proceed, what to do, how to ask. What if she ovulated early? Her body was faulty, there was no telling if it would stick to the fourteenth-through-sixteenth-day rule. She felt as though every second counted, that there wasn't a minute to spare.

Oh, Lord, the more she thought about it, the more she became stressed. Could he see that in her eyes? Her fear? Her desperation? Her impatience?

He touched her hair, her cheek. "Relax," he said softly. "We have time."

She should have known he would read her emotions. She bit her bottom lip, finally gathered the courage to look at him.

"I feel so weird," she admitted, forcing a laugh. "I know we're going to make love and I'm suddenly as shy as a virgin." She flicked her hair behind her ear. "Should we go in…?" *And get right to it,* was what she didn't say.

"Is that what you want?" he asked softly.

"Darn it, I don't know. It's just that I'm afraid of missing a moment…the moment that could be the right one."

"If you're tense, focused on only that thought, your body will likely work against you."

"How do you control thoughts that haunt you like an obsession?"

He looked deep into her eyes, slid his hand around to cup the back of her neck, drew her closer. "Let's try this. Don't think for a while. Just feel."

He touched her lips with his, gentle yet sure. Her heart lodged right in her throat, stuttered, then pounded with a vengeance.

He's an absolute expert at this was her fleeting thought an instant before her mind went blessedly blank. There was only this man, this single, spine-tingling kiss. His tongue swept the seam of her lips, yet never entered her mouth. He simply toyed with her lips, nibbled, worshipped, caressed them with his, slowly, magically, as though they had an eternity.

He held her with only the slight pressure of his hand at the back of her neck, his palm so wide it wrapped around to gently cup her cheek, his thumb sweeping the line of her jaw, back and forth. It was a simple touch, one that might have soothed, yet it inflamed.

When he eased back, she moaned, blinked away the sensual fog. He slid his palm down her arm, took her hand and linked their fingers.

"Come. Let me show you my world."

It took her a minute to catch up. He meant his ranch, his life's work. She felt a pang of remorse. She only planned to be in his world temporarily.

"But I thought—"

"I know. We might be on a mission here, but there's no reason we can't take a little time to make it special. Get to know each other. Build trust."

"I trust you."

He brushed back a strand of hair that blew in her face, stuck to her lips. "Humor me, then. I'm a little nervous."

She gaped at him, astonished. Then she saw the amusement in his eyes. He wasn't anything of the

kind. He was flirting with her. Wooing her, she realized, stunned.

He was giving her the opportunity to relax, lulling
her into that easy, dreamy state where bodies began
to hum and sensations dictated the rules.

Rules that consumed body and mind, steeped a
person in intimacy and left no room for worries over
conception.

She swallowed hard. The very self-assurance of
this man was an aphrodisiac. "Well, then. I guess
we can't have you being nervous."

He tugged the brim of his hat. "Guess not. Are
you okay like that, or do you want to change?"

If they went their separate ways to change clothes
she was terribly afraid they'd lose the momentum of
the spellbinding excitement that arced between
them. Her ivory broomstick skirt was easily washable, as was the vest that buttoned over her lacy
camisole. And beneath all that, waiting like a present
to be opened, was what she considered man-
stopping underwear. She'd worn it for a reason—to
feel feminine on her wedding day, to give her confidence.

And by dog, she wasn't taking it off until it had
been seen and appreciated.

"I'm fine," she said.

He nodded and, keeping her hand in his, walked
her around the grounds closest to the house. The sun
was setting, a beautiful time of day, when heat from
the sun-drenched earth mingled with the cooler air
of dusk. Soft winds had smeared wispy clouds
across the sky in a pastel finger painting of color
that drew the eye and the breath. Wind chimes tin-
kled in the breeze, creating a melodious chorus be-

hind the harmony of insects and the various sounds of animals settling.

A funny sensation shivered inside Eden. Peace. Safety. A sensation much like a lingering, cherished memory—like how the smell of peaches always evoked instant images of her grandmother's kitchen, the counters lined with crates of fruit fresh from the orchard. Every summer, without fail, they'd gone to the peach orchard. It was a part of their life, a constant, a ritual. Something to count on.

And for some really odd reason, Stony's ranch evoked that same sort of sensation.

She cautioned herself not to get caught up in the fairy tale but to guard against vulnerability. He was only her temporary husband. This was only her temporary home.

He was doing her an enormous favor. And she wouldn't embarrass either of them by letting him know that her feelings ran deeper. Much, much deeper than she'd planned.

Foolish, she thought. She'd gone into this with her eyes wide open, knowing that when the time was up, the marriage license they'd signed would molder in a file cabinet somewhere, perhaps even end up in the trash barrel.

But that was months away. In the meantime she would hoard as many memories as possible. Someday, God willing, she would have a child. A little boy or a little girl with Stony's lips, his amber eyes, his strong jaw.

And his gentle way.

The memories she built now would evolve into stories to tell her child; their child, a means of keeping Stony close at heart and a vital part of their baby's life, even though opposing life-styles separated them.

Stony's fingers squeezed hers. "You're deep in thought."

"Mmm. Just thinking about families, parents." *Me and you.*

They stopped in front of Henry's stall, and Stony reached over the wooden door to give the horse's cheek a scratch. Touching came so naturally to him.

When images of him touching *her* threatened to buckle her knees, she knew a distraction was in order. "Tell me about your grandmother."

He released her hand to check the latch on Henry's stall door. "She was a remarkable woman. I see her in every corner of this land, in the flowers by the back door, that old cypress down by the creek. I see her out here in the barns, remember the special, gifted way she spoke to the animals, using only touch and body language."

With a hand at Eden's back he led her a little way down the smooth cement aisle that ran through the center of the stable.

"The sorrel over here was hers," he said, reaching up to pet the elegant horse that immediately came to greet them, poking her head out the stall door. "Her name's Penny."

"Oh, she's a beauty." Eden reached across the half door to rub the animal's neck. Her coat was a cross between a deep gold and a reddish brown, with a matching mane and tail. For an instant Penny stood proudly and gave a dainty bob of her head. Then her ears drooped and her nose dropped toward the ground, her chin nearly resting on the wooden gate, as though Stony and Eden were family and there was no call to put on fancy airs in front of kin.

"For the longest time I worried that her heart was broken," Stony said softly. "Did you see how she perked up and stood so tall when we came? She's still looking for my grandma, watching for her. That head bobbing she just did was her way of getting a better look around—just in case Grandma was standing directly in front of her. She wouldn't want to miss that."

"I don't get it."

"Horses have a small blind spot in their field of vision—just in front of them."

"Oh. I beg your pardon, Penny." Eden moved a step to the side, gazing into Penny's huge, velvety eye. "I'm so sorry I'm not who you expected." Penny's head raised a bit. "How can you tell if she's sad?"

"Her ears'll droop."

"Oh, no." Eden reached up to touch Penny's relaxed ears. "None of that, now." Like a star pupil anxious to please, the horse's ears pricked and her head came up a notch.

"I'll be damned. You're the first person she's actually responded to without ten minutes of coaxing."

"You're kidding. Not even Nikki?"

"Especially not Nikki." His mouth turned up at the corners, and Eden realized he'd let down his guard, wasn't even aware of the expression. "Nikki's a little…energetic for Penny's liking. This lady stands clear when Nik's in the area."

Eden laughed. "I don't blame her. Nikki could worry the horns off a billy goat." Lest he think she was criticizing she quickly added, "The sign of a healthy, happy, five-year—"

Her words arrested in her throat when she turned her head. Stony's arm was braced high against the wall beside her, his head bent at the perfect angle for kissing. He was so close she could feel the warmth of his skin radiating through his cotton, snap-front shirt. When he swallowed, his Adam's apple bobbed beneath the brown bandanna tied at his throat, and Eden had the most pressing urge to bury her lips just there.

He raised his brows, clearly a gesture that translated into a silent question. A knowing gesture that made the question moot. Yet he asked, anyway, "What?" Softly, so softly. His thumb swept across her bottom lip, and his gaze fastened right there for several exquisitely arousing seconds.

"I forget," she whispered.

Those incredible amber eyes shifted lazily from her mouth to her eyes, and Eden feared she would hyperventilate right there on the spot. Her heart pounded, and her breath came in shallow pants. Every pulse point in her body was attuned to his, called to his…begged.

To heck with trust and wooing and getting to know each other, she was good to go, right this very minute.

But for a man who read body language so expertly, he was doing a dismal job with hers.

Stunning her right down to her toes, he straightened and took a step back. "Ready?"

"Do you even have to ask?"

The left corner of his mouth tipped upward in the sexiest smile she'd ever seen. She blinked, made fists with her hands because they were trembling like mad.

"I meant to resume the tour." The smile reflected in his voice.

"The…" Did she have to conk him over the head, here? Surely her ability to convey sexual signals wasn't *that* rusty. "Uh…no. That's not strictly what I'm ready for."

"What then?"

"At the risk of repeating myself, do you even have to ask?"

"It'll be dark soon." He took her hand, obviously to get them moving.

She tugged, stopping him. "What does dark have to do with anything?"

He gave her that steady look again, his thrillingly sensual eyes so riveting she couldn't have looked away even if someone yelled fire.

"It's hard to tour the ranch after dark." He brought her knuckles to his lips. "As for you, I'll want lights. Plenty of them."

She blinked. Her skin was on fire even as chills raced up and down her arms. He'd kissed her hand. *Her hand.* Nobody had ever done that.

"Stony, in my upbringing, a girl being forward with a boy is…well, it's just not done. And I'm sorry, but I'm going to toss teaching right out the door and say it plain out. I'm ready to go inside. To bed. Or—" she gestured around her "—the hay's fine by me."

"Do you realize how expressive that Southern accent is? It'll drive a man to his knees."

"Well then, feel free," she blurted out, her mind consumed with that incredibly seductive image.

He actually laughed. "We'll get there. Right now, I think I'm still a little nervous."

"Right. And that horse over there is going to sprout wings and a horn and fly through the barn." She'd never felt such keen sexual frustration.

He shook his head. "That'd be a shame. Owner's got a lot invested in that Thoroughbred."

She took a breath, gathered her wits, felt her smile tugging. "All right. But if the engine won't warm up again, don't say I didn't warn you."

About to take a step, he stopped, looked down at her. "I guarantee it'll warm up." His voice was deep and filled with masculine confidence. Not the kind of confidence that was off-putting, but the kind that tapped right into a woman's fantasies.

Especially Eden's. This was a man who would not need, nor ask for, a performance-rating in bed. The excitement brought on by that realization nearly made her stumble.

Despite his gentle hold on her hand, she untangled her feet and her mind and fell into step beside him.

Warm up, ha! She was going to overheat and likely catch fire.

She needed a distraction. Desperately.

"You mentioned your grandmother was deaf. But she spoke?"

"Not often. The sound of her voice drew stares of pity from other people, and she was the least likely woman to be pitied. She was strong and brave, with a heart that could reform an ax murderer."

Eden smiled. "That's a very powerful gift. She raised you?"

"From the time I was thirteen."

"And before that? Or would you rather not talk about it," she said quickly.

"I don't mind. This is the 'getting to know you' I promised."

He'd promised her much more, but Eden didn't want to get sidetracked again.

"When I was eight, my folks and I were on our way to a horse auction when the axle on the trailer broke. Dad had been reaching down on the floor for something, so he wasn't prepared. The trailer jack-knifed, then we just started flipping."

"Oh, Stony, how horrible for you."

"Yeah. I walked away with only bruises. My parents died on the spot."

Oh, no. He'd witnessed that as an eight-year-old boy.

"The paramedics took me to the hospital in Jackson—"

"Mississippi?"

"Wyoming. My parents were dead, and the authorities couldn't seem to locate a next of kin. I told them about Grandma, but I didn't know her last name. Only that she lived on a ranch in Montana."

"She was your mom's mother."

"Yes. Let's walk." With her hand in his they stepped out into the twilight, slowly traveling the path that led to the back door of the ranch house.

"I felt really stupid that I didn't even know my own grandmother's last name. The people from the state promised they'd find her, but in the meantime they had to do something with me, so they sent me to a boys' home. I kept telling the other kids I wasn't staying, that in a couple of days my grandmother would come for me. And when she didn't, they needled me. The dumb big guy. Even at eight I was a lot taller than the other kids.''

Oh, she hurt for him. "Children can be so thoughtless." She tightened her fingers around his palm, hugged his arm to her side, feeling his hard biceps press against the swell of her breast. "You said the accident happened when you were eight but that your grandmother had raised you from thirteen on. You were in foster care for five years?"

"Looking back, it seems incredible. As the days passed and my grandmother didn't show, I figured she just didn't want the responsibility of me. Turns out she didn't have a phone. She couldn't hear, so she considered it a frivolous expense. With no phone and a different last name from mine, it took a while for someone to notify her of my parents' deaths." He shrugged. "One of those freak things where paperwork falls between the cracks."

"More than paperwork," she said softly.

"I suppose the state of Wyoming was pretty embarrassed that they'd let procedure and human decency slip through their fingers. By that time—nobody would actually own up to responsibility—I was stuck in the system, almost like they'd forgotten me."

"Surely they told your grandma that you'd survived the accident?"

"Yes. They told her." His jaw tightened as did his fingers on hers. "But some idiot who'd obviously never heard of discrimination laws arbitrarily decided that Grandma's handicap made her unfit to raise a child—never mind that she'd raised my mom just fine. Grandma fought for information and action, but she wasn't getting very far. I'd been moved to another home, and mysteriously the paperwork disappeared.''

"You didn't ask about her in all that time? Bug the case workers to keep looking?''

He shook his head. "I thought she didn't want me. I was stubborn. I wasn't going to set myself up for more rejection. I was getting enough of that as it was.''

"But she found you,'' Eden said softly.

"Yes. And just like the way she gentled the horses, she had to gentle me. I was pretty angry.''

Eden hugged his arm harder and rested her head against his shoulder. "Did she sue?''

"No. Didn't believe in it. But she was happy to track down the people who'd appointed themselves judge and jury and got them fired.''

"Good for her.'' Eden was indignant on his grandmother's behalf. They were at the back porch now, and Eden turned, placing her hand on his chest, over his heart, unconsciously rubbing. It was a trait she'd inherited from her mother. In sadness, Beverley Williams would gently rub right there over the heart, her way of soothing, of healing.

"You've lost a lot of people close to you.'' She was also thinking about Nikki's parents, friends obviously close enough to name him godfather of their daughter.

"But the replacements I got,'' he said softly, "Grandma and Nikki, have been the best things in my life.''

Still, Eden could only imagine the pain. She'd never experienced the death of a loved one. She was blessed to have both her parents, four grandparents, aunts, uncles and cousins—most of them living right outside of Dallas, like her.

She realized she'd taken that for granted lately.

He smoothed her hair behind her ear, then placed his hand over hers, holding it to his chest.

She felt his heart thud beneath her palm and knew hers matched the rhythm, and still he simply gazed down at her.

"What?" she asked.

"You're so beautiful. I can't imagine why men aren't breaking down your door to sweep you off your feet."

She gave a wry chuckle. "Not likely."

"But there *have* been relationships."

"Yes. Nothing serious, though." She shrugged. "Most of 'em kissed with their eyes open."

Stony jolted, raised a brow. "Unforgivable," he murmured wryly, amusement lighting his eyes.

"Unromantic," she clarified.

"Seems yours would've had to be open, too, to notice."

"Guess that means the guys weren't too special, huh?"

"I guess," he echoed, staring at her. Watching her. "So, how do you like to be kissed?"

Her cheeks instantly warmed, and her vocal cords seized. The cicadas sang in the trees as fireflies blinked yellow among the daisies as though providing the color hidden by night. "Um…you do a fine job."

His knuckles grazed her cheek. "Do I?" His head lowered, stopping a breath away from her lips. "Your eyes are open," he pointed out.

Oh, Lord. She thought she might faint. She'd

never met a man who made her feel like this. "Yes. So are yours. But it feels romantic with you."

"Mmm. Close your eyes."

"I might miss something."

"I guarantee you, sweetheart, you won't miss a thing."

And she didn't. Her whole body became a hive of nerve endings, her senses so keen she felt every single one of them—individually and all at once.

Incredible, she thought. Magic.

She reached up to caress his face. His hand followed, circled her wrist, gently tugged her hand down. For a moment she came back to earth, felt a flash of coherency amidst the maelstrom of exquisite sensation, and realized he was preventing her from touching his scar.

She leaned back, took his face in her hands, and drew him down within easier reach, holding his gaze. Slowly she closed her eyes as though savoring the finest, most mouth-watering dessert, and softy, very softly, pressed her lips to the scar that had become invisible within five minutes of meeting Stony.

"You are a beautiful man," she whispered. "Someday you'll tell me about this wound. But not right now."

He swore, his voice deep and raw with emotions she could only guess at. Wrapping his arms tighter around her, he snatched her to him, kissing her in a way that made her mind go blank and her body pulse with pleasure.

She met his aggression, matched it and took them even further.

He reached behind her, yanked open the door,

maneuvered her into the kitchen and up against the counter without ever breaking the kiss.

She came up for air. "I take it our tour is over?"

He bunched the hem of her skirt in his hand, drew it up her thigh, pulling her leg up with it. His palm swept up the back of her thigh, paused over the garter and the top of her stockings, then slid higher, over the firm, naked swell of her behind.

Stunned, Eden sucked in a breath.

With her feet barely touching the floor, she felt the hard length of his arousal against her pelvis. Urgency pounded in every fiber of her being.

She pressed against him as the edges of reason blurred, as appeasing the torturous ache deep inside her became the paramount goal.

His head lifted, his amber eyes nearly black with desire. His fingers traced the band of her G-string panties.

"If I'd known what was under this skirt, our tour would have been much shorter." His fingers grazed her inner thigh, wrenching a moan from her. "Baby, we need a bed. Fast."

Chapter Nine

He swung her up in his arms and strode toward the stairs. Eden's whole body trembled in anticipation and excitement. No man had ever carried her. It was a fantasy she'd been too shy to ask a partner to fulfill. Perhaps she hadn't trusted the others.

Stony made it seem effortless, made her feel petite when she was pretty much average.

She'd been in his bedroom before, tidying up. It was a no-frills room, wood floors softened by area rugs, a king-size bed covered in a patchwork quilt.

All male. Just like the man looking down at her, the utter intensity of his gaze making her giddy.

Stony lowered her feet to the floor and undid the shell buttons on her vest, surprised by the tremor in his hands. It wasn't visible, thank God, but he could feel it.

Her skin was soft and warm and smelled like a dream. She had a face that caused heads to turn, a body that brought to mind perfection. More often than not, her green eyes smiled in fun and hinted of sex. An odd and potent combination. A rich tumble of red hair framed a milky-white complexion the Montana winds would likely play havoc with.

She was a study in the perfection of femininity.

A perfect beauty in his eyes.

And he couldn't believe he was the lucky guy who got to make love to her.

He slipped the vest from her shoulders, then hooked his thumbs in the waistband of her skirt and slip, kneeling as he pulled the garments away.

His breath caught, and he took a minute to rein in his control. The sight of her in ivory silk, lacy garters, sheer stockings and a tiny scrap of material masquerading as panties nearly knocked him senseless.

Her fingers flexed in his hair as he pressed his lips to the silky camisole covering her belly. He wondered if she was imagining his baby there.

He filled his hands with the firm swell of her behind, squeezed, molded, drove himself nuts. He wanted to rush, yet he'd promised himself he'd savor.

He intended to draw a response from her that would make her forget that her goal was to get pregnant.

He wanted her to want him. Madly.

He wanted her surrender.

He was giving her his seed, and he desperately, foolishly wanted her soul.

And if he wasn't careful he could blow it, unconsciously hold too tight. With horses, he was well aware that he had to first earn their trust, while always allowing them room to flee should they become uncomfortable.

The same applied to Eden. He didn't want to trap her. Butterflies should be free. The problem was, he realized with a pang, he truly wanted to wrap this butterfly in a cocoon and hold her to his heart forever.

As though reverently opening a coveted present, he slowly lowered one of the sexy lacy garters, letting it drop to her ankle, then smoothed his palms back up over her calf, to the top of her thigh, all the way up to the minuscule elastic band of her barely-there panties.

She sucked in a breath when his finger lingered. He paused, glanced up to make sure she was still with him, that the sound was desire rather than the product of being ticklish.

Desire. Definitely.

He turned his attention back to her hosiery and rolled an ivory stocking down her leg, something he'd never had the pleasure of doing to a woman except in his fantasies. Her skin was as soft as the silk covering it. She steadied herself with a hand on his shoulder as he lifted her foot and pulled off first her boot, the garter decorating it like a hat tossed drunkenly over a lampshade, then the delicate stocking that puddled at her ankle. By the time he'd dealt with the second leg, he was nearing combustion.

He stood, slipped the tiny strap of her camisole off her shoulder and pressed his lips there, working his way up her neck, nipping her ear where a creamy pearl pierced the lobe. He felt her shiver and tremble, and wondered if she could feel the same reaction in him.

Her nails dug into his back, and she squirmed against him. ''Stony—''

He covered her lips with his, nibbled at them, kissed the dimple in her cheek, the corner of her eye, the delicate skin of her temple where fine blue veins reminded him of her fragility, of how the waning of her health had scared the hell out of him less than a week ago.

"I know we've got a purpose, but that's no excuse to hurry." His thumb swept over her pouty bottom lip. "This isn't going to be fast."

He saw the stunned arousal in her eyes as she accurately read the sensual promise—or threat—in his tone.

"Um, maybe we could negotiate on that point?"

His lips canted and he felt the damned scar pull at his skin. But right now he didn't care. With Eden, it didn't matter. The shallow breaths she drew told him everything he needed to know about her emotions, the level of her pleasure.

It wasn't nearly high enough.

"Not this time."

"Then, could we at least even the score a bit?" She untied the bandanna at his neck, ripped open the snaps on his shirt, spreading the panels, feverishly running her palms over his chest.

For several mind-numbing moments, Stony couldn't move and he couldn't think. It felt as if the top of his head was going to come off.

And, man, what a great way to go.

Avid lips caressed his throat, and pert, silk-covered breasts rubbed erotically against his chest. He was a man about to go down for the count, rendered mindless by a siren with soft hands and clever lips.

If he didn't take back control—fast—his self-assurance over his skills as a patient lover would be nothing more than hot air.

He whipped the silky camisole over her head,

then took her face in his hands, automatically bent his knees to even their heights and kissed her long and deep, the inside of his forearms scorching where they rested against the sides of her breasts.

He had every intention of sticking to a plan, a slow buildup, but Eden suddenly locked her arms around his neck, plastered her body against his and poured so much eroticism into the kiss that he lost all reason.

He tumbled her onto the bed and yanked his arms out of his shirtsleeves. Their hands tangled at his belt, each suddenly in a big hurry to feel skin against skin. He won the struggle, got the zipper down and kicked off his jeans.

Need clawed like a savage beast in his chest, his heart racing like a Thoroughbred's crossing the finish line.

But they weren't at the finish line, he reminded himself in a moment of sanity.

My God, what was he thinking? He was twice her size.

Her little moan of pleasure nearly sidetracked him, as did the undulation of her pelvis against his arousal. He wrapped a hand around her hips, stilled her erotic motions. Her eyes were closed, and he felt a little clutch in his gut. He tried to ignore it, but memories intruded.

Paula had only made love with her eyes closed—with him at least. He'd thought it was ecstasy. She'd set him straight on that before she'd walked out the door.

"Eden, look at me."

Eden fought her way out of the sensual bliss that was about to wring her dry. Something in Stony's tone, though, reached out to her. Surely he didn't intend to stop. If he didn't put out this fire raging through her, she was certain she'd crumble like the edges of a charred cookie.

"I'm looking," she whispered. With her hands, she framed his face, ran her thumbs over his lips. "You're not going to ask me to kiss with my eyes open are you?"

Whatever had caused his hesitation seemed to have passed. Now a smile lingered in his eyes. He was obviously remembering their conversation, the yardstick by which she measured the sincerity in a partner.

"What if I do?"

"Depends. Are yours going to be open, too?"

"I wouldn't want to miss anything." His words echoed her earlier ones.

"Then I suppose I'd need some sort of reassurance up-front that your mind wasn't otherwise engaged."

He ran a finger down the center of her chest, circled her breast, rubbed his thumb over her nipple, his eyes following the movement. Then he looked back at her.

"Baby, when I touch you, with or without my eyes open, there's no room for anything else in my mind but you." His lips replaced his thumb.

Eden sucked in a breath, chills of arousal prickling over her body. "In that case...oh!" His teeth scraped over her nipple at the same time his palm slid between her legs, cupped her. "Carry on," she finished weakly.

And, oh, my gosh, did he ever. Need built, so hot, so immediate, she wasn't sure what to do with it, how to process it. She wanted more, but couldn't find enough air in her lungs to tell him.

No amount of writhing or urging would get him to hurry. He took his time, simply kissed her, worshipped her body, paid homage to every inch of her skin. He took her to peaks she hadn't known she could reach, then gently brought her down and started all over again.

It could have been hours, minutes or days that passed. The one and only thought in Eden's mind was to have him inside her before she fainted dead away or died from pleasure and anticipation.

"Now, Stony. Cryin' out—oh!" She sucked in her breath, felt his weight shift over her, felt him press right against the core of her, the place where she throbbed and ached, wanted him the most.

With his fingers threaded through hers, he pinned her arms to the bed, letting his elbows hold the majority of his weight up off her.

And as he slid his body slowly, carefully into hers, he watched her.

She couldn't have looked away from him if her life had depended on it. Breath held, gazes locked, she tried to isolate each sensation so she could go over it in her mind later when she'd regained her wits.

But that was impossible. Too many sensations and emotions crowded at once.

He took from her, yes, but he gave so much more in return. It was as though his entire being was focused solely on her pleasure. And Eden knew it was selfish, but she couldn't seem to do anything to even the score. She could only feel, flying on the wings of a desire that scorched her from the inside out.

He let go of her hands and slid his palm beneath her hips, tilting them up to meet his thrust. Slowly, in and out, then with increasing speed.

Legs bent, heels digging into the mattress, she lifted her hips and met him, matched him, urged him farther, higher, harder.

"Wait," he said.

"Not a chance." She intended to take everything he could give her, and at last had the wherewithal to return the pleasure. In a frenzy of need, she kissed his shoulder, his neck, his jaw, everywhere she could reach and pressed her body into his, giving a subtle move that had him groaning and swearing.

She felt her body clutch, again, wondered if she could live through another climax. She might have screamed. She wasn't sure. There was nothing slow and easy about the orgasm that gripped her. Violent spasms contracted her muscles, clutching him tighter inside her. Bliss burst in a kaleidoscope of brilliant color behind her closed lids as she felt him grow incredibly harder, heard him whisper her name an instant before his seed emptied inside her.

EDEN'S SKIN WAS SLICK with perspiration, as though she'd taken a dip in a swirling hot tub. The breeze from the window tiptoed across her cooling flesh, making her shiver and burrow closer to Stony's side.

She wasn't sure her heart would ever recover its normal pace. Beneath her palm she could feel Stony's heart keeping a close race with hers, could see the pulse at his solar plexus visibly palpitating the taut skin of his flat belly.

She was stunned by the tumultuous emotions he'd wrung from her. She'd come here expecting a sexual relationship, naturally figuring it would be awkward at first, take a little practice to get comfortable with each other.

It was nothing of the kind.

Her body still tingled and pulsed. She'd never been made love to like this, so thoroughly, so carefully, so...*well*. Her world had been rocked.

This, she thought. This is what she'd searched for all her life and had never truly known how to define. It had been an elusive dream, blurred around the edges.

But Stony had crystallized the image for her, bringing those edges into sharp focus.

He was safety and gentleness. Virility and capability. A man with principles that wouldn't allow him to consider an affair when an impressionable little girl was in the house.

A strong man, in character and in strength.

A man a woman could lean on and trust. A man who knew exactly who he was and didn't apologize for it or boast about it.

A man who would never, ever let a woman fall.

But for all that, for all the tender care he'd taken with her, it was hard to remember that he was merely doing her a favor.

Attempting to give her a baby.

And that confused her. Because tonight had *not* been about getting pregnant. It was too intense. It was the wrong time of the month.

So what had it been?

Earthshaking, that's what. But she wouldn't embarrass either one of them by reading more into it than just great sex.

Incredible sex.

"Thank you," she whispered, frowning when she felt the muscles of his chest tense.

Realizing her words had unintentionally reduced what they'd just done to strictly clinical, she rolled on top of him, propped her chin on his chest and grinned.

"I meant for the orgasm."

"Just the one?"

"Uh, no. I was saving you a swelled ego by not admitting I'd lost count after the second one."

His hand slid over her back, up and down. "Five."

"Hmm?" She'd laid her cheek against his broad chest, the lazy sweep of his fingertips lulling her.

"There were five."

Her head jerked up. "You were counting?"

"A man's interested in these things."

He looked so pleased with himself. And well he should be, but that was beside the point. She laughed. "How ungentlemanly of you. I told you your ego would get involved."

"More than my ego's involved." He cupped her behind, shifted her, rubbed her against his growing arousal. "Want to try for ten?"

Never had a deep, rugged voice and bold words seduced her so quickly. She squeezed her legs together, savoring the sweet, achy throb that had her hips shamelessly undulating against him. "I don't know…" Her voice was breathy, aroused. "I'm not sure I could survive that much stimulation."

In one smooth, erotic move, he rolled with her, kept his hand on her butt, tucked her hips under his and kneed her legs open, fitting himself between them.

She sucked in a breath, read the intent in his eyes. "You'll survive."

"Oh, yes." She locked her legs around him and made it to number six before he'd even completed the second thrust.

By MIDNIGHT Eden finally hollered uncle. The bed linen was on the floor, and she was worn nearly to a frazzle.

"I need sustenance." She was on top this time, feeling like a limp rag doll. "Did we even eat tonight?"

"Do the burgers we had at Brewer's this afternoon count?"

She glanced at the bedside clock. "Technically that was yesterday. But we can count it if you like, because I have a major craving for ice cream." Something icy-cold to give her a little respite from the heat. Her husband had the stamina of five men. But Eden wasn't complaining. She, too, had plenty of staying power. Who knew she'd have such an insatiable sexual appetite? It had obviously been hiding all these years and was making up for lost time. "I'm thinking peanut-butter swirl."

"Do we have peanut-butter swirl?"

"Of course. Vera ordered it in special."

"Then we'd better satisfy that craving of yours."

The sweep of his palm over her hip sent a thrill shooting through her. She laughed and pecked a kiss on his lips. "Not that one, sugar."

Stony watched as she crawled off the bed and walked naked to his closet. By all rights his body ought to be spent. The sight of Eden's bare backside shot that theory all to hell.

She disappeared into the walk-in closet and came back out wearing one of his shirts, raising her arms to free her long hair from the collar. Her breasts lifted with the action and Stony swallowed an agonized groan. He didn't know whether to swear or thank God when she pulled the panels of the shirt together and snapped it closed.

She looked up at him, raised a brow. "Well?"

It would be in his best interest to get up. Because if he didn't he was going to drag her back down in this bed with him. And much more of this wild pleasure would likely kill him.

He debated for several seconds. He would certainly die a happy man, that was for sure.

Finally he swung his legs over the side of the bed and stood, having the extreme, ego-boosting pleasure of watching her jaw go slack as her eyes fastened on his body. His aroused body.

"What do you expect?" he asked. "Hard not to react when a beautiful woman's looking…intently, I might point out."

"How very rude of me." Her gaze lifted—reluctantly, it seemed. "Did I mention I flunked my deportment class?"

He loved it when she went all properly Southern on him.

He walked toward her. "Teacher must have been blind. Not a thing wrong with your behavior." He ran a finger down her cheek, lightly brushed the back of his hand over the slope of her breast, then bent and picked up his jeans that were crumpled on the floor, where he'd kicked them off several hours ago. "A little wild…but I like that in a woman."

"Cryin' out loud."

Her voice was breathy, aroused. Stony swallowed hard and pulled on his jeans, not bothering with shoes and a shirt. They were like heat lightning together, electricity arcing between them when they so much as brushed.

He knew better than to be acting like this. They were married only because he'd made it a stipulation.

They were making love because Eden wanted a baby.

The sexual chemistry was threatening to make more out of this than was there. He had to be careful.

Ah, to hell with careful. He'd been careful all his life.

He was temporarily married to a beautiful woman who'd given him free rein with her body. A woman who reveled in her sexuality and had no reservations about showing it.

A man's fantasy.

A dream.

And for as many nights as he had her, he was going to enjoy her. They might be using each other, but there was no reason not to take advantage of sex that was so hot it threatened to combust.

From behind, he hooked an arm around her waist, lifted her to his hip. "Come on, wild thing. Let's get you fed."

She giggled, made a token protest at being hauled around like a sack of grain. Her bare feet dangled a foot off the floor, her bottom rode the button of his jeans, and her soft, pert breasts rested against his forearm. When she wiggled against him, Stony wrapped his other arm around her waist and buried his lips in her neck.

This woman was like a drug in his system.

She reached back, put her hand at the back of his head and encouraged him to continue. "Mmm," she murmured. "Call *me* wild thing, will you. Have you looked in the mirror lately?"

For a split instant, his arms tightened, his insides going still. He couldn't help it. The reminder of reflections in glass twisted his stomach.

Get over it, guy.

Scraping his teeth over her earlobe, he ground her derriere against the rigid arousal behind the fly of his jeans, torturing himself, determined to coax that little breathy sound of surrender that she invariably made so prettily, so easily.

Her responsiveness was a soothing balm and a giant boost to his ego. His hand slid down to cup her, the tails of his shirt that she wore creating a thin barrier between his fingers and her feminine heat.

She moaned. "Stony..."

"Uh-uh. Ice cream first." He eased her down the front of his body until her feet touched the floor, but kept his hands at her waist, preventing her from turning. Because if she turned, he knew damned well he'd haul her right back to that bed.

"You are a very bad man."

"And you are a very *good* woman."

She smiled, walked forward at his urging. "You're fishing for a reciprocal compliment."

He let her precede him down the stairs. "To a man, bad is the highest compliment."

She glanced back at him, licked her lips.

"Good…because I like that in a man. A little bit bad. A little bit dangerous. Know what I mean?"

There was invitation in that sassy look, the kind any man would recognize and drop to his knees to kiss the ground in thanks for.

The kind of look that told him he could have her body and do *anything* his heart desired.

"Stick your head in that freezer, wild thing. We both need a break here."

Chapter Ten

Stony figured he was the one who ought to stick his head in the freezer. The tantalizing sight of Eden wearing only his shirt, the hem hiking up as she reached for a carton of ice cream, kept his body on slow simmer.

"I wonder if Nikki's having a good time with Ian," Eden said as she took bowls down from the cabinet and scooped large helpings of peanut-butter swirl into them.

"I imagine they're asleep."

"Mmm, I imagine." She set the dishes on the table and sat down, licking a drip of ice cream off her knuckle. "I miss her."

Stony picked up his spoon, hesitated for just a moment, searching for signs of subterfuge. It was a knee-jerk reaction, and he was ashamed of himself. Especially since all he saw in her open face was honesty.

"It's only been a few hours."

"You can't tell me you don't miss her, too."

"I do. Every time she's out of my sight I'm conscious of it. That little girl has my heart."

"Oh my gosh." Holding her spoon aloft, she put her free hand over her chest. "That is so touching."

No, he thought, it was just fact. But Eden's expression was so classically female, so classically mushy, he smiled. The scarred skin beside his eye pulled, and he automatically compensated.

"How come you do that?"

"Do what?"

"Stop yourself every time you're about to smile."

"I don't."

"You do." She laid down her spoon, propped her chin on her hand. "Will you tell me how you got that scar?"

Ah, hell. For long periods of time he could forget that it was there. He avoided mirrors unless they were absolutely necessary—like when shaving. His looks disgusted him, but that was no call to slit his throat.

"Eat your ice cream."

"I am." But she didn't even attempt to pick up her spoon.

Stony shoved away his bowl and leaned back in the chair. "It's no big deal."

"Then it shouldn't bother you to talk about it, should it?"

"Are you always this tenacious?"

"I wouldn't be here if I wasn't."

Yes, it took tenacity and a fierce, *fierce* desire for her to pursue this pregnancy, to risk the odds, to go so far as to marry a stranger to get what she wanted. What she *needed*. She wasn't a woman to give up easily.

"I got it in the explosion that killed Nikki's parents."

"Oh, no."

He nodded, realized it had been a long time since he'd talked about his friends. That wasn't right. He needed to keep their memory alive. For himself. And especially for Nikki.

"Dani and Nick Langly were high school sweethearts, my neighbors and very close friends. I was an impromptu midwife when Dani went into early labor out on a cattle drive."

"She went on a cattle drive in advanced pregnancy?"

"Ranch wives are different from other women." When Eden raised her brows, he added, "In my experience."

"Which is fairly limited, I might point out, since the older folks in town are convinced there's a lack of females around here and are dragging women in off the highway."

"Not exactly off the highway." He smiled. She had a point. He hadn't known a lot of women who'd been pregnant or given birth. "Dani thought she had a month to go, that's why she'd insisted on manning the chuck wagon. When she went into labor, Nick lost it. Never mind that he knew as much about the birth process as I did—which was only based on animals—he just went into a tailspin, and I ended up delivering the baby."

He absently rubbed his chest. "Most incredible thing I've ever done in my life." He glanced up at Eden, saw the compassion on her face, the interest, the way her hand was unconsciously pressed over her womb...the yearning. And he suddenly hoped like hell that he could give her the miraculous experience of giving birth.

"They asked me to be Nikki's godfather, and there was no way I could refuse—or that I'd want to refuse. It was as if she was mine. I'd wanted a family and thought I'd get one when I married Paula. But Paula kept saying she wasn't ready. So Nikki was like my surrogate kid. There was a special bond between us."

He raked a hand through his hair, then leaned forward and rested his elbows on his widespread knees.

"I visited the Langly ranch a lot—as much, I think, to see and hold Nikki as to visit with my friends. That's what I was doing that day. As well as being territorial over the chuck wagon, Dani was an attorney and worked out of an office in the house so she wouldn't have to leave the baby. Nikki's second birthday was coming up, and between work and party plans, Dani had a lot on her plate, and that day she'd been especially relieved when I took Nikki off her hands. We were in the tack room and Nick and Dani kept brushing up against one another. I decided to give them a little privacy."

He shifted in the chair again, restless, feeling raw, as though the nightmare had taken place yesterday instead of three years ago.

"One minute I was standing outside the barn holding Nikki and the next thing I knew an explosion had taken the top off the barn and knocked me several feet away. Thank God my body was big enough to shield Nikki from the debris hurled by the blast. That's how I got this." He tapped a finger at his brow.

"Oh, Stony. How awful for you."

"The cut was the easiest part. I didn't even feel

it. The hard part was listening to Dani's voice as she repeated Nick's name over and over. I could hear her pain and fear, knew by her tone that Nick was already gone. I called to her, told her I was okay, that Nikki was okay, and that I would come for her, to just hold on. When she heard me, she just started screaming. God, I'll never forget it. Save the baby, Stony! Get her out. Get her out. Get her out.'' He closed his eyes, repeated the words even as he heard them echoing in his head—in Dani's voice. "She thought I was still inside the barn."

His eyes snapped up when Eden threaded her fingers through his, squeezed hard and held on. Her strength surprised him. Her genuine compassion made his stomach flip. He squeezed back, then released her hand. He wasn't used to compassion, didn't totally know how to accept it.

"I tried to get them out. God, I tried. I handed Nikki off to one of the ranch hands who'd come running at the sound of the blast. But I couldn't see. There was blood in my eyes, and smoke and flames formed a barricade between me and any hope of making it back inside." His voice lowered. "By then Dani's voice had gone silent." For all his size and brawn, he'd felt so totally inadequate. Even now he could hardly bear to think what kind of pain she might have been in, how she'd suffered.

He took a deep breath, shook off the memories. "So, that's it."

"Did you find out what caused the explosion?"

"Linseed oil on some rags that got kicked too close to the pilot on the water heater."

"You should never hide that scar, Stony, or be

self-conscious. It's your badge of courage and honor.''

"I wasn't courageous. I couldn't save Dani and Nick."

"But you saved Nikki."

"Luck. She was in my arms."

"And you shielded her with your body, nearly got yourself killed in the process, I imagine. And it took great courage and honor to uphold your promise to Dani and Nick. You're an exceptional father, Stony. Your friends would be so happy and proud."

He wasn't comfortable with her praise, yet at the same time he reveled in it, wanted to be heroic in her eyes.

She fidgeted in her chair, made circles in the melted peanut-butter swirl with her spoon. "And Paula…what happened between the two of you?"

"Now there's a subject not worth a lot of time. Paula married me because I had money. I met her at a horse auction. She was beautiful, classy and pure plastic." He shook his head. "Too bad I didn't see that sooner. Would have saved me a million bucks and—"

"Wait. Back up. Did you say a *million* dollars?"

He barely nodded. Watched her. She was astonished, yes, but no ghoulish dollar signs lit her eyes.

"You've got that kind of money, and you insisted on signing a prenuptial to protect *my* catering company's assets from *you?*"

"It was good business sense."

"Well. I guess I won't lose any more sleep over splitting the company coffers." She waved a hand. "My mouth's closed now. You can go on with your story."

It gave him a punch that she so easily spoke about their pending separation—even though her tone had been wry. And he was annoyed that he was bothered by the reminder. After all, the time limit had been his suggestion.

"Paula hated it here in Shotgun Ridge. She didn't fit in. She dressed inappropriately for ranch life and she was bored out of her mind. Every chance she got she'd hitch a ride to the city with Wyatt or Ethan or Ethan's brothers—who all flew planes. One thing Paula was good at was shopping."

"What in the world kept y'all together?"

"Sex."

She blinked. Opened her mouth. Closed it. Nodded. "I don't believe we need to go into details about that."

He wouldn't have, anyway. "So when I took Nikki in, Paula packed her bags. Said she hadn't signed on for kids. She wanted money and she wanted out. Told me I wasn't sophisticated enough for her tastes."

Eden's hand came down hard on the table. "Are you joking?"

He smiled. Her indignation on his behalf made the nasty subject a little easier. "Nope. She wanted a guy who wore tuxedos and drove a Jaguar. Hell, I couldn't even fold myself into one of those things. At first she thought my money would make up for the drawbacks. Turns out it didn't." She'd told him he was an exceptional lover. That's why she'd stayed two years—because he made her crave sex like an addict craves drugs. That at least had been a salve to the slap...until she'd turned the slap into a blow by telling him she'd had to keep her eyes closed—especially after the explosion had ripped apart his face. That little zinger had cost him some pride.

Paula taught him his personal limitations. Money could only buy happiness for a little while. And good sex couldn't hold a person forever.

In hindsight he wondered if the sex had really been all that good with Paula. She'd been okay in bed, a little selfish. She craved the pleasure he could give her but rarely returned it. She didn't get involved, didn't run her hands and mouth and body over him until he couldn't remember his own name, didn't shoot his control to hell and back, didn't drive him mad with a sexy-as-sin Southern drawl.

"Paula was a shallow witch," Eden said. "You're better off without her—though I'm sorry she took your money." How awful for him. Rubbing salt in the wound. Eden couldn't imagine anyone acting the way Paula had.

Looking at Stony, she was hard-pressed to keep her libido under a boil. His chest was wide, his stomach flat. A physical man in excellent physical condition. And he looked so sexy sprawled in that chair, shirtless and shoeless, a pair of well-broken-in jeans molding his thighs and cupping his sex. She nearly groaned.

"Thanks for worrying over my bank account."

Eden thought she detected a smile in his voice, but wasn't sure. This man didn't show his cards often. "I don't give a fig about your bank account. I was thinking about you. A million dollars seems particularly nasty."

She stood and picked up the two bowls swimming with foamy melted ice cream, rinsed the dishes and bent over to put them in the dishwasher. Her bedroom was in her line of vision, and she wondered if she should sleep there for the rest of the night—or morning, rather. Would she be presuming too much if she went back to Stony's room?

Stony swallowed a groan when Eden bent over. The shirt had ridden up just high enough to tease.

He watched her walk back across the room, looked up at her when she stopped in front of him. She drew in a breath that had her breasts lifting.

"Something on your mind?" he asked. He hoped they were done talking about the past. Rehashing tragedy and failure had a tendency to tie a knot in a man's gut. Even now, emotions were raging inside him, a turbulence that had no outlet. At least, not for a few minutes yet.

He saw her glance at her room and realized what was making her skittish all of a sudden.

"Don't even think about it," he said. She stood next to him, a dish towel in her hand, the tails of his shirt hanging to her midthigh, her legs very close to straddling his knee. He knew she didn't have a stitch on under that shirt, and he went from zip to hard in three seconds.

She exhaled, and he saw relief. She wanted him, but was obviously minding her Southern manners lest she appear greedy.

Stony didn't have any such problems with manners. Greedy was good. Something about Eden Williams brought out a different side to him, an insatiable aggression.

He stood, crowding her, watched the flush of desire spread over her chest, up her neck. Her lips were parted, and those wide green eyes were so expressive.

He smiled slowly. "Sugar did that ice cream do anything to revive you?"

"Well...I'm—"

"Too late." He hooked his hands around the backs of her thighs, lifted her onto the table and stepped between her spread legs. With his eyes spearing hers, he reached for the snap of his jeans, pulled down the zipper and stepped out of the pants.

"Ready?" he asked softly. "Or not?"

Here I come, Eden's mind finished silently. His words were a blatant, exquisitely thrilling sensual threat.

Eden swallowed hard. "Yes," she whispered.

"Yes, what?"

"I'm ready."

His hands rubbed a lazy path over the tops of her thighs, his thumbs skimming the insides, coming very, very close to where she was naked and most vulnerable...arousing, teasing.

And all the while he studied her. A look so exclusive—dangerous even—she shivered.

"I want you so bad right now, Eden. And I want it fast. So if you want to cry uncle, now's the time."

She shook her head, could hardly speak. Anticipation and desire shot through her with such force, she experienced a scary and appalling moment where she feared she might swoon.

"Then hang on tight, baby." He ripped open the snaps of her shirt.

Her breath caught. Oh-oh, here was that danger she'd teased about upstairs. *I like that in a man,* she'd said. *A little bit bad. A little bit dangerous.*

She trusted him completely, but that didn't stop the tiny sexual thrill of fear from rushing through her veins. She'd had no idea Stony Stratton would be so unpredictable, so unrestrained, such an expert, self-confident lover.

He hadn't even started, and her desire was already over the top, her nerves singing with the same urgency she saw in his face.

With one hand on the center of her chest and the other supporting the back of her shoulders, he laid her down on the table, then yanked her hips to him and her legs around his waist as he thrust into her.

Eden's back arched off the table. Her lungs wouldn't take in enough air, or maybe it was too much. She didn't know. She only knew that this was utter, glorious bliss. She would surely go down in the record books for the most climaxes in a single wedding night.

He pulled her up to a sitting position, his hand under her long hair, cradling the back of her head. The tender hold was in direct contrast to the carnal way their bodies strained and fused.

She felt herself tumbling over the edge, felt the mind-numbing clutch of her body that signaled the squeezing, uncontrollable spasms of pleasure.

Suddenly, with his hands under her bottom, he lifted her off the table, took a couple of steps back until his shoulders slammed up against the wall.

Her legs clenched tighter around him. "Wait! Can this…?" *Work,* was what she would have asked.

It wasn't necessary. He *showed* her how well it worked.

With a strength, skill and speed most men couldn't have pulled off on a bet, he kept them both upright and worked her body exactly the way he wanted, the way she needed, the way she craved. Urgency radiated from every pore, every squeeze of his hands as he raised and lowered her on his steel-hard body, thrusting faster, higher, breathing heavier.

He maneuvered her body as though she weighed no more than a saddle, and all she could do was hold on for the incredible ride, let the astonishment and pleasure roll over her in wave after frenzied wave of ecstasy.

Just when she thought she couldn't take another second of the blissful gymnastics, when each breath she desperately sucked in and exhaled came out as a scream, he thrust high and hard, and shouted her name. With strong fingers, he gripped her hips, ground their bodies together, holding her still, his manhood pulsing, pulsing, pulsing inside her, touching her womb and clear through to her soul.

For endless moments he stood there, leaning against the wall, her legs around his waist, his forearms effortlessly supporting her weight, his face buried in her neck, both of them breathing as though they'd just run a ten-mile race.

"Who won?" she finally whispered. Her breasts, slick with perspiration, slid against his heaving chest.

"I'm for calling it a draw," he said.

She nodded. "I could sit still for that."

She felt his lips curve against her neck. "Say my name."

"What?"

"Just say it."

"Stony."

"I love the way your accent changes the sound of the *o*. Gives it a twang that makes me hard."

If she'd had the energy, she would have smiled. "I'll remember that."

"Do that."

Her inner thighs were slick with sweat, and she squeezed them tighter to keep from slipping. If asked to stand on her own two feet right now, she didn't think she could manage. Stony shifted his arms more securely beneath her, and she dropped a quick kiss of thanks on his forehead.

When their chests weren't heaving quite so hard, she asked, "Have you ever considered that *you're* the one with the accent, and I'm the one who speaks correctly?"

"You hear anybody else in town talking in a sexy drawl?"

"I don't know. I haven't met everyone in town."

"Pretty close. You're outnumbered. And darlin', I hate like crazy to admit this, but I need a bed. I think I'm done for the night."

"As long as it's just for the night." She'd meant it in teasing. She realized her mistake at the same instant his muscles went rigid beneath her hands.

Sex had clouded the fact that they had a goal to accomplish. And the odds were definitely better if they spread it out, consistently, day after day instead of all at once.

Two more weeks, give or take a few days, and her period would come again—unless they were very, very lucky and his seed and her egg were as combustible and compatible as they were.

Part of her prayed like mad that's what would happen, that a baby would grow in her womb, sending the debilitating adenomyosis into remission, beating the Grim Reaper and the surgeon's knife.

And the other part of her wished for a little more time. With Stony.

As though reading her thoughts, her confusion, he tenderly pressed his lips to her temple and carried her back upstairs, her legs around his waist, naked bodies spent yet still locked together.

EDEN HAULED AN ARMLOAD of clothes on hangers up the stairs. She was sure she hadn't arrived with all this stuff in her two suitcases. Obviously she was more efficient at packing than she'd given herself credit for.

She turned the stereo up loud to keep her company and couldn't help pausing by the window in Stony's bedroom—again—to look down on the ranch. Regardless of turning her emotions inside out until the wee hours of the morning, he'd gotten up as usual—and left her body humming.

It was the darnedest thing how she'd suddenly become this insatiable tigress in bed. She'd been good to go again this morning just feeling his weight shift in the bed.

But he hadn't taken her up on the invitation. He had work to do, horses to feed and groom and train.

So much for a honeymoon weekend. She might as well go on over to Hannah's and pick up Nikki.

She huffed out a sigh. After all that, the man just up and went to work.

"Oh, stop it, Eden," she said aloud, then reflexively glanced around to see if anyone had heard her—which was absurd since she knew she was alone.

Besides, Clint Black's voice belting from the stereo was loud enough to reach her just fine upstairs, so even if there was somebody in the house, they wouldn't have heard her mutterings over the volume of the music. Aptly—or not so aptly—good old Clint was singing about what was on his mind when he'd said "I do."

Honestly. She hugged the armload of clothes to her chest. There was no call to expect Stony to treat the weekend like a honeymoon; to stick by her side. He hadn't married her for love or even for the long haul. The sole point was to try and get her pregnant.

And Lordy, if last night was any measure of what was to come, her reproductive system would have to be dead—and her along with it—for it not to jump right up and snag one of those coveted sperm.

Unbidden an image of the sunny room on the east side of her house in Dallas popped into her mind. She could see it so clearly—a fanciful mobile hanging over a white crib, fluffy blankets draped over a rocking chair, toys peeking out of a lacquered wooden box stenciled with cartoon animals, shelves on the walls filled with storybooks and piggy banks and keepsakes.

Realizing what she was doing, she shut her mind to the images, afraid she would jinx something.

Walking into the room-size closet, lined with fragrant cedar, she pushed aside Stony's jeans and shirts and hung her clothes next to his. Draped across the hamper was a pair of white cotton men's briefs, a scuffed brown boot lay on its side and a wide leather belt was coiled on the floor like a snake. Otherwise the closet was fairly straight. It wasn't stuffed with clothes, and there weren't a whole bunch of things crammed on the shelves.

In fact, there was quite a bit of noticeably empty space—shelves that would hold racks of shoes, a ton of drawers that would take two solid weeks of shopping to fill, and clear plastic bins void of odds and ends.

The size and design of the closet was the only hint that this hadn't always been only a masculine room. Elsewhere there was no trace of the woman who had once shared it with him. After hearing about Stony's ex-wife, though, Eden wished her good riddance, glad there were no reminders of the evil woman.

She hummed along with Vince Gill as she put her creams beside Stony's in the bathroom, hesitating when she set the box of feminine unmentionables beneath the counter. Now they were in all four of the bathrooms.

Her stomach clutched and fluttered as she imagined herself not having to touch a single one of those boxes for the next nine months.

With a hand pressed to her abdomen, she left the bathroom, determined to keep busy and quit torturing herself with what-ifs and if-onlys.

The cedar chest at the end of the hallway held an absolute treasure trove of wonderful things—glass bowls, a candy dish and a bobby pin holder in mint-green and pink carnival glass, delicate teacups and saucers, a silver-backed hairbrush and mirror set, a bowl and pitcher wash basin with a hairline crack along one side of the bowl.

Carefully she hauled her cache back to Stony's room and set about to soften the stark masculinity in the decor. Besides, she'd always felt that masculinity was all the more evident when contrasted with a few frills. She ran her fingers over the beautifully embroidered hummingbirds hand stitched on a table scarf, then laid the fragile cotton on the cherry wood dresser and arranged her perfume bottles atop it.

Satisfied that she'd gotten everything transferred from the downstairs room to Stony's, she picked up her recipe box and went to the kitchen, lowering the volume on the stereo as she passed.

She needed the mindless act of cooking to keep her thoughts off Stony, her body and her womb.

Perhaps she would get a head start on the week's meals, put together a couple of casserole dishes. Then there was that new recipe for Danish pastry she wanted to try, and Nikki had adored the cookies with faces made of M&M's. Maybe she'd whip up some of the sticky buns Hannah had nearly swooned over. And if she made those, she might as well do up a batch of the scones Dora had politely said were good enough to give her an orgasm.

She was up to her elbows in flour when Stony walked in the back door, automatically ducking as he passed under the jamb.

Her heartbeat slammed into high speed, and her blood sizzled. She ran her tongue over her bottom lip and watched Stony's eyes flair.

So much for cooking taking her mind off sex.

He studied her as though waging a debate. A not wholly pleasant one, judging by the frown lines on his forehead.

Then he dragged his gaze away and looked

around the kitchen, brows raised. "Cooking a few things?"

Using the back of her wrist, she swiped at an itch on her cheek. "My mind gets carried away sometimes." Stopping to look at the disorder in the kitchen through his eyes, she grinned. "Despite actions to the contrary, I really am a focused person and run a very efficient, successful business. It's just that I start thinking about several things at once and I end up with two or three projects going at the same time. Thank goodness I finish what I start."

"Always?"

Oh, my gosh, the look of purpose on his face and the implied sensuality in his deep, gravelly tone made her knees go weak and her tongue stick to the roof of her mouth. He wore the white hat that was as much a part of him as his deep-chocolate hair.

Good guys wore white. Lord, she had no idea where that thought had come from. Right now, though, he didn't look anywhere close to good. He looked big and bad and highly motivated to have his way.

She swallowed hard. "Usually."

He took off his hat, tossed it on the granite countertop, then slowly, deliberately, came toward her, his whiskey eyes trained on her like tractor beams. "Make any exceptions?"

"Um…I imagine I could. Do," she amended quickly.

His smile was that of a predator, and Eden was astonished. The man was like night and day, depending on which side of the door he was on. Outside—on the ranch or in public—he was soft-spoken, a deep pool of still water, a gentle man who

kept to himself yet would give a stranger his shirt—
or his seed, in her case.

Inside, in private, he was danger and excitement,
thrillingly improper and bold, a sorcerer and a ma-
gician when he put his hands on her body. A man
with a masculinity and sexuality hot enough to burn,
and cool enough to surprise.

He didn't even give a courteous pause or a passing wave to her personal space as he invaded it,
eased right up against her and kept on going. His
thighs molded to hers as he walked her backward
toward the bedroom off the kitchen that she'd just
spent half the afternoon moving out of, his mouth
toying with her lips, her cheek, her ear.

With a hand at the small of her back, he pulled
her tighter against him, tight enough to let her feel
the thick line of his arousal.

She opened her mouth to suck in air, and he filled
it with his tongue, effectively and immediately
sweeping her brain clean of coherency or reason.
The power of his kiss whipped through her, lit her
desire quicker than the hot, blue flame from a
burner.

Flour sprinkled over his shoulders like snow
flurries as she locked her arms around his neck,
rubbed against him as though she could climb right
in his skin.

He groaned, buried his lips in her neck, cupped
his hands over her behind and lifted her. Aligning
their bodies for maximum torture, he ground her
against his arousal—hard.

She felt cool tiles against her back, opened her
eyes and realized they were in the bathroom. He put
his knee between her legs, exerted enough pressure

to lift her slightly and pinned her against the wall using merely his bent thigh and his pelvis to hold her there. His hands were braced high on the wall behind her, his breathing as heavy as hers.

"What are you doing to me?" he asked.

Although she imagined it was a rhetorical question, she turned it around on him. "Since I'm the one with my feet off the floor, I'd say you're doing it to me."

His lips curved. "I didn't plan on this. I just came in for a snack."

"And the sight of a woman with flour in her hair sends you into fits of lust?"

"Evidently." His hand lightly brushed her hair, and his thumb swept the side of her face.

"My gosh, do I have the stuff all over me?" She must look a sight.

"Not *all* over." He pulled her T-shirt up to her armpits, reached between them and undid the snap of her shorts. "You smell like a sugar cookie. I want to eat you up."

She sucked in a breath. "Sometimes I don't know what to do when you say things like that."

His tongue skimmed up the side of her neck. "I know. And it drives me wild when you get that little catch in your voice, when your drawl gets heavier and your breath goes soft." He lowered his knee, allowed her feet to touch the floor, pushed her shorts down until they fell around her ankles on their own.

Eden shoved her hands under his shirt, felt his skin prickle with chills of desire and his nipples go hard under her fingers. "So, what are we doing here?"

He chuckled. "If you've gotta ask, I'm doing

something wrong.'' He stepped back so that her hands dropped away, gripped the hem of her T-shirt and pulled it over her head. Then he shrugged out of his own shirt and reached in the shower to turn on the water.

''I'm going to take a big bite out of you, baby— partly because you smell like a mouth-watering bakery, mostly because I damn well *have* to.'' He unhooked her bra, took a moment to taste the upper swell of her breast. ''I've got a problem, though. I smell like a horse, but I don't want to wait for dessert. Seems I've become a slave to my appetite, and I'm in a dilemma.''

He had them both naked before she could even register the process. Wrapping his hands around her rib cage, he lifted her until her face was level with his.

''Anything gonna burn in the kitchen?''

She shook her head, still back at the part where he'd said he was going to take a bite out of her. *You smell like a sugar cookie. I want to eat you up.*

''Good. In the interest of speed and my lack of control, you're gonna have to get wet.'' He stepped into the shower with her. ''But I promise I'll make it worth your while.''

Chapter Eleven

Stony figured two weeks would have taken the sharpest edge off his desire and put a rein on his thoughts so he could at least give his work his full concentration.

He'd figured wrong. All he could think about was finding some excuse to go back up to the house, to check on Eden. She'd been looking tired the past few days, and it was starting to worry him.

He latched Fox-Trot Dandy's stall and hung the lead rope in the tack room, happy with the stallion's progress. They'd developed a trust, grudging on Fox-Trot's part at first, but the bond had eventually solidified. He wasn't biting anymore and was nearly bombproof. Even through the report of a pistol, the Thoroughbred would stand with disciplined, military precision, wouldn't even flinch unless Stony gave permission. That's what came from using a soft voice and an easy touch. From asking for good behavior rather than insisting. Hopefully the proud beauty would behave as cooperatively for his handler and jockey.

Leaving the barn, he made his way around the corner of the house, then paused and stepped back in the shadows. Eden was on the porch, both her guitar and Nikki in her lap. A couple of his employees leaned against the wooden rail with adoring looks on their faces.

Jealousy zinged through him, and at the same time his heart kicked and flooded him with the familiar desire.

That beautiful woman hugging his daughter and entertaining his friends was his wife.

And what kind of spell was he under that kept making him forget that their marriage license was only a formality, her presence in his bed merely a means to an end?

He had to remember that she didn't need him. She had a full life waiting for her in Texas—a home of her own, a successful business, friends, family.

She only needed what he could give her.

So now he had the right to make love to this gorgeous woman whenever he wanted—which had been every night for the past two weeks, from the time Nikki went to bed until well past midnight.

But only at night.

The restriction was the only way to keep Stony focused on reality. The reality that this arrangement wasn't permanent.

Her laughter drifted on the afternoon breeze, wrapping around him like a down comforter on a cold winter's night. She dropped a kiss on Nikki's head, called her doll baby in that sexy Southern drawl, then quickly plucked the strings of her guitar and began to sing, "Ten bottles of milk on the shelf."

Stony chuckled when Eden sang *milk* and Nikki, Demone and Marcus all sang *beer*. Her palm slapped across the six strings, stopping the tune, and she gave a mock admonishing glare that sent Nikki into peals of laughter. Rosie leaped across Demone's foot and licked Nikki's face, quivering in excitement at the prospect of the gigglefest turning into a full-out romp that she could participate in.

Despite the gaiety Eden projected, Stony noted the strain around her eyes. With her bright smiles, easy conversation and nimble fingers on the guitar strings, she was doing a pretty good job of fooling everyone around her—everyone but him.

He saw her get up, place her guitar in Nikki's lap and excuse herself. He pushed away from the barn wall and followed her.

"Gentle with the guitar, Nik," he said quietly as he mounted the porch steps, passing Marcus, who was on his way down. "Just like with the baby horses."

"Okay, Daddy." Her little hands opened so that the guitar was just sitting in her palms—in danger of falling to the ground.

He squatted, placed his hands over hers, showed her with actions the amount of pressure to use—just like his grandmother would have done with him.

"When you finish being a rock star, why don't you and Rosie go to the stable with Demone and spend some time with the pony so she won't get lonely." He glanced up at Demone who nodded, understanding that he had kid duty for a bit.

Demone had been on this ranch longer than Stony had, and from the day Nikki had come to live with them, he'd been as territorial over the little girl as Stony and Grandma. Stony knew he wouldn't mind.

As Stony expected, the reminder of the Shetland

pony he'd imported from Britain a couple weeks ago was a lure Nikki couldn't resist. If he would let her, she'd take Rosie and sleep in the stall with the little horse.

"I better not be a rock star anymore 'cuz Pony's ears might not like it," she said as she gently balanced the guitar on his knee and waited until he'd gotten a good hold on the neck before she let go.

Stony agreed, but kept that to himself. Nikki's underdeveloped vocal cords made her sound like a wolf with laryngitis baying at the moon. But what she lacked in singing skills she made up for with sheer exuberance and volume. And that would definitely annoy the hell out of the little Shetland who was still adjusting to her surroundings, still new enough that Nikki had yet to settle on a proper name other than Pony.

Stony exchanged another look with Demone. Assured that Nikki was in good hands, he rose and went into the house to check on Eden, to see if his suspicions were on target.

The bathroom door was closed, and it took everything in him to wait patiently for her to come out. He knew she rarely locked doors—he'd found that out the first week she'd been here when he'd accidentally burst in on her. For the first time in thirty years, a blush had stained his cheeks, and he'd immediately slammed the door.

Eden had handled the awkward situation better than him. When she'd come out, she'd laughed away his stammering apology and told him she'd lived alone for so long she never thought to lock the door. With dimples creasing her cheeks, she'd told him he was lucky she even remembered to *close* the door.

Well, the door was closed today. And the longer it stayed that way, the tighter his muscles bunched.

To hell with it. He raised his hand to knock, but his knuckles never touched the wood.

The heartbreaking sound of her sobs breached the mahogany-stained oak and speared right into his heart.

Damning propriety and privacy, he twisted the knob, strode across the room and scooped her right up off the low tile wall at the front of the tub.

Startled, she instinctively fought him.

"Easy, baby," he said softly, and cradled her in his lap as he sat on the closed lid of the commode.

With a shudder that ripped a piece of his heart, she fisted his shirt in her hand, curled into his chest and wept.

He closed his eyes, swallowed hard. "Shh. It's okay. I've got you."

"I'm sorry," she whispered.

"No need to be sorry."

Her breath hitched, and he tightened his hold on her, the sound of her tears cutting him to the quick.

"I promised myself I wouldn't do this. That I wouldn't get my hopes up." Still gripping a wad of his shirtfront, her fist pounded against his chest, punctuating each agonized sentence. The blows were featherlight, expressing pain rather than inflicting it. "They've been riding high since that first day...after the wedding."

He laid his cheek on the top of her head. "I know." Neither one of them had expected the wild, incendiary chemistry that had flashed between them from the onset, a craving need they fed on voraciously night after night.

Truthfully, it had been in the back of his mind, too, that by right of sheer quantity—*quality* quantity—they'd have immediate success.

But with success would come an end. Could that intrusive thought have been subconsciously undermining their bodies? His?

He buried his lips in her hair, rocked her, could feel her using every bit of her waning strength to get a hold on her emotions. He felt so damned inadequate, didn't know what to say or what not to say.

He'd seen her longing every time Hannah had stopped by, the awe when she'd placed her hand on Hannah's swollen stomach. And he knew what these monthly cycles did to her, both mentally and physically.

Even if it meant that she'd go away, that he'd lose her, he wanted to give her what she desperately, genuinely yearned for.

A baby in her womb.

A chance to experience a miracle.

"We've got time," he said.

With her cheek still resting on his chest, she looked up at him, nodded, her eyes red-rimmed and vibrantly green. He smoothed damp auburn hair back from her temples, swept away the tears that bathed her face, leaned down and gently kissed the corners of her eyes, her lips, kisses that had nothing to do with arousal and everything to do with healing.

Fresh tears welled in her eyes, and Stony could taste the agony in the back of his throat. Hers and his. "Oh, baby, don't."

She gave a watery laugh. "Pitiful, isn't it? A grown woman over thirty without the slightest control over leaky eyes."

He passed his thumb over her bottom lip, over the slight dimple peeking out of her cheek. "Naw. I think there's a rule somewhere that says women don't have to give a fig about control or feeling weepy."

She sniffed. "Cryin' shame Eve had to pluck that doggone apple."

"Mmm, hmm," he murmured idly. "If she was here, I'd hold her down so you could slap her."

Her spontaneous laugh was a cross between a sob and a hiccup. She shifted in his lap, wrapped her arms around his neck and hugged. Hard. He expected the pressure to ease within about two seconds and was surprised when it didn't, when her arms continued to squeeze. Steadily. Tightly.

He placed his palm between her shoulder blades, gently patted, felt the silk of her long hair slide against his fingers and over his forearm. And still, without the slightest pressure from his hand keeping her there, she clung.

Something in his chest thumped, as though a padlock had just clicked open. No woman had ever held on to him like this, like she wanted to crawl right inside his skin and stay there, like he was her lifeline, her hero.

Then softly, so softly, she whispered against his neck, "Thank you, Stony. You are a very, very special man."

He closed his eyes. *But not special enough for you to stay.*

EDEN PICKED UP THE PHONE, knowing she had to call Carrie and check in. Lately, she'd been forgetting about her business, and that wasn't fair to Carrie, especially since her partner was being good enough to carry the entire load while Eden pursued pregnancy.

"Garden of Eden, Carrie speaking."

"How's it going, Mugs."

"Eden! You're worrying me to death, I'll have you know. How come you haven't called?"

"I did. Last week, remember? And the phone works both ways, pal."

"Yes, but I'd hate to interrupt the *honeymooners.*"

"So don't call me in the middle of the night."

"What, those boys out in Montana haven't caught on to the joys of making love in the daylight?"

Eden took a breath, leaned her head back against the pantry door. Every night she and Stony made love like greedy teenagers, passions raging nearly out of control. And sometimes it was easy to forget that they weren't like most other newlyweds. They touched, explored and whispered words that bordered on love yet were carefully interpreted as pleasure.

But in the light of day, they were more like roommates. He did his thing and she did hers. And subtly, not unkindly, Stony kept a shield between them.

Out of nowhere a lump formed in Eden's throat, and she had no idea why. It was just that lately she'd found herself yearning to hold hands in public, wished she could at least sit with Stony on the sofa, drape her legs over his thighs, have him pull her into his lap, his big, capable hands hooking around her thighs and holding her tighter to him as they watched some sappy movie on television. Just that.

Not sex.

Romance.

As though they were truly married.

A foolish, foolish yearning.

She knew why their intimacy rarely extended past the bedroom. It was the only way each of them could hold back a piece of themselves, to pretend that they weren't in over their heads, that when the time came, hearts wouldn't be completely broken.

And with the intoxicating power of desire that flashed between them—night *and* day—holding back was darn near killing her.

"Eden? Dang it, I'm an insensitive jerk. I didn't mean to tease. I know how important this is to you."

"Hey, I'm fine."

"Are you sure? You went all quiet on me, and you know how I get when people aren't talkin'."

Eden grinned. "Mugs, folks usually can't get a word in edgewise with you."

"Oh, see there? I try to be sweet, and she calls me a motor mouth."

Eden laughed. "So how's tricks?"

"Jumpin' like frogs on a hot skillet."

"But?" Eden asked, having known Carrie long enough to pick up on undertones.

"You'd have just died," Carrie said dramatically. "We had to do this hideous kids party up in Highland Park. They wanted everything purple, and I mean everything. The cake, icing, spaghetti…well, you get the drift. I used a case of food coloring and blueberries. The whole thing was terribly tacky, Eden, especially for such a ritzy neighborhood."

Eden laughed. "I bet you were up to the task. How about the servers?"

Carrie groaned. "Remember the California raisins doin' a little dance to 'Heard It through the Grapevine'? That was us. Purple makeup on our faces, purple spray in our hair. Took me three washings to get the junk out. And the worst part of the whole thing was the little party girl was a brat."

"Ah, you poor thing. How was the pay?"

"Profit city. That's the only saving grace. Of course, I inflated the bill outrageously."

"Shame on you."

"*Purple* hair, Eden. Think about it."

Eden laughed. "Yeah, I guess that is pretty bad. Wish I'd been there to see it."

Hearing a sound at the doorway, she turned and smiled at Stony. "Hang on a sec, Carrie." She put her hand over the mouthpiece of the phone. "Did you need me?"

Oh, that sounded wrong. Like a proposition in broad daylight. Besides the fact that they didn't *do* daylight, she was on the phone. Then again, the sight of Stony Stratton in tight jeans, sexy leather chaps and a Stetson pulled low over his brow was enough to give her a hot flash.

If he said yes, she was terribly afraid she'd drop the phone and forget all about Carrie. And that would never do. Carrie would have a field day primly reminding Eden that good girls were taught to have a little restraint, to exercise a little decorum.

To preserve her dignity, she quickly amended, "I meant—"

"I know what you meant," he said quietly. For several charged seconds his gaze didn't waver.

Eden was used to him speaking quietly, used to his intense looks, but there was something different about him today. She frowned, wishing she could read him as easily as he seemed to read her most of the time.

Her palm was still over the phone, and she wondered if he thought she didn't want him to listen to her conversation. Before she could tell him she didn't mind, he shook his head and said, "Just passing through. Didn't mean to interrupt."

When he went by her on his way to the back door his scent swirled around her. Leather, fresh air and masculinity. A very potent combination.

"Eden? Are you still there?"

A bit dazed, she lifted the phone to her ear and tore her eyes away from Stony's behind as he disappeared out the door. "I'm here."

"What's the matter with your voice?"

"Carrie, have you ever seen a cowboy in chaps?"

"Sure. Over at the honky-tonk in town."

"No. I mean a *real* cowboy. Dusty scuffed boots, chaps buckled low on the waist and tied high at the thigh, the leather worn and dirty from saddles and horses, jeans that mold to the man so perfectly you can *see* which side of the fly his—"

"No!" Carrie shrieked in an oh-my-gosh-tell-me-more tone.

"Yes. Clearly."

"John's doesn't show like that."

"John wears baggy pants."

"Maybe we'll go shopping for jeans tonight. I wish I knew what this Marlboro Man of yours looks like."

"He's not really mine," Eden said on a sigh. But

she was really starting to wish that he was. "Ask Aunt Lottie. She'll show you a picture."

"I just might do that. Do I still have to dodge the judge?"

Eden laughed. "No. Mom's cool about the whole thing—sort of. She said if I wasn't home by Christmas they were coming out."

"Well, that'll be cozy. Oh, dang it. They shipped me the wrong oil again. Jennifer!" Carrie hollered. "Catch that delivery guy."

"Sounds like you're busy," Eden said. "So I'll let you go."

"Are you okay?" Carrie asked. "Need money or anything?"

"I'm fine. You call me next time, okay, Mugs?"

"Will do. Just not at night," she teased.

STONY WAVED as Vera Tillis carried a paper sack out of his kitchen, put it in her truck and drove past him.

Eden had been baking again. No, *again* wasn't the right word. *Still* was more like it. And he would bet money that Vera had delivered a load of supplies from the store. It was starting to bother him that he never saw a bill or any extra charges on his account.

Seemed a lot of things were bothering him lately. But damn it, she wasn't paying for one more load of groceries, never mind that she'd practically opened a coffee and sweets shop right in his kitchen.

And there was the other rub. It had only been a little over a week since she'd cried in his arms as though her heart had broken, breaking *his* heart, damn it, then spent several days in pure agony as her life seemed to drain right out of her before his very eyes.

Scared the living hell out of him is what she'd done.

He kicked dirt off his boots by the back door. Watching her suffer so bravely had been bad enough the first time—before the ceremony. This time it had been worse. Maybe because of the intimacy; maybe because the stakes were higher—health versus a baby and one unproductive month already used up. He didn't like feeling so damned helpless when she grew so weak.

And it had *really* annoyed him when she'd suggested she go sleep back downstairs during "her time." He gritted his teeth. She hadn't wanted to disturb his rest. Did she think he could sleep knowing she was practically bleeding to death? Did she think he could just close his eyes and not worry that she'd passed out on the floor or something?

He stared at the back door, wondered if he should just skip lunch. He was in a mood, felt as though there was something right behind his sternum that was about to bust out. He didn't mind all these people stopping by for coffee and rolls and stuff, but he worried that Eden was going to overdo. She was so stubborn.

And she looked so damned *right* in his kitchen, entertaining his neighbors, blending in as though she'd lived here all her life. But she hadn't. And she wouldn't.

I wish I'd been there to see it. Her words were still echoing in his head from yesterday.

There was his problem, he knew, the reason he

was feeling like a mustang with a burr under his blanket.

She'd been talking to her business partner. A reminder that he wasn't a long-term husband. Just the stud.

He raked a hand through his hair. That sounded nasty, even in thought. He would like to think he was a little more than that. A friend, at least. A friend she just happened to have a wild, insatiably incredible sexual relationship with. Even now, watching her move so effortlessly, so familiarly around his kitchen was giving him a hard-on.

Hell, he was pathetic.

Giving his jeans a tug, he walked into the kitchen. Eden smiled and Iris beamed. "Stony!"

"Hey, Iris." He saw the plateful of scones and raised his brow. "Changing the menu at Brewer's?"

"Actually, I've been trying to steal your wife away."

Wife. He breathed deep and lifted his gaze at the same time Eden did. Her eyes skittered away. They both knew that less than five months from now, he'd be left to explain why he and his *wife* were getting a divorce.

"Since she won't come cook in my kitchen," Iris said, "we've arranged for her to be my dessert supplier."

Stony looked at Eden. Did she really have any business baking trays of goodies for the neighbors when she'd barely had time to recover her strength? She worried him, damn it. Even though she'd given him the green light to do so, he hadn't made love to her last night—not because it wasn't a critical time of the month but because she'd still looked a little tired to him, fragile.

Iris stood and picked up her plate of scones. "I'd best be getting back to town."

"Don't let me run you off," Stony said.

"You're not. I like to keep close to the phone now that Hannah's time is so near." She kissed Eden, then Stony. "Thanks for the goodies, Eden. I'll call and check on you tomorrow."

Stony opened the back door and watched until Iris got in her car. Then he turned back to Eden. "You shouldn't be working so hard—so soon."

"I keep telling you, cooking's not work. It's therapy." She held a carafe over the cup on the table by the place setting she'd laid out for his lunch. "Coffee?"

He nodded and sat down, noted that she'd folded his napkin like a swan and set it in the middle of the plate. She was always doing stuff like that, dressing up the table with flowers and linen and all manner of special touches.

He kept seeing more and more of his grandmother's treasures around the house, things Paula had hated and Grandma had packed away in order to accommodate her and make her feel that this was her home, too.

He hadn't realized how much he'd missed some of these things—fussy teacups and lacy scarves on the dressers. Stuff that had memories attached to them.

He ran his hand over the rose-patterned tablecloth, scooted away the fluted bowl filled with cherries that Eden had set in the middle as a centerpiece, and smiled.

"I remember the day I burned this hole in the tablecloth."

"Burned?" Eden asked as she set a turkey sandwich in front of him and sat down.

"Yeah. Wyatt and Ethan dared me to strut through the house with a cigarette between my fingers."

"Why?"

"Hell if I know. Why do kids think up half the stupid things they do? I made it all the way into the kitchen, then heard my grandma coming out of the laundry room. It didn't even occur to me that she could have smelled that smoke a mile away. Her senses were really keen. I dove for the flowerpot on the table, missed and put the butt out right there on the tablecloth."

"What did she do?"

"Nothing at first. Her hands were full of towels. It was her eyes, though, kind and disappointed, amused even. I sat right down and waited for her to come back and give me what for, even though Wyatt had his nose pressed to the screen door and Ethan was advising me to make a run for it."

He pushed the bowl of cherries back over the ragged hole. "I expected a whole lecture—and at that point I hadn't totally mastered sign language, so I wasn't sure I'd be able to keep up. But she just cupped my chin and asked me if I *wanted* to smoke. I said no, and she smiled and signed, 'That's good, but if you do, please use the outdoor plants or ash cans to extinguish your butts, and leave my lovely violets be.'" He shook his head. "Took all the fun out of sneaking around, if she was going to give me permission to do it."

"I imagine she knew that," Eden said, reaching across the table to pour mint iced tea in his glass, even though he hadn't touched his coffee.

"Yeah, she did. You don't have to serve me. In fact, you didn't have to fix lunch for me at all. I can do it myself."

"Don't be silly." She scratched at a spot on the tablecloth with her thumbnail. "I like doing stuff for you."

It was a wonder he didn't choke on the sandwich he'd just bitten into. She was talking about serving him a meal, and he was interpreting it in a sexual context.

He concentrated on mentally counting the number of stalls in the barn and naming each horse in order.

"Stony, can I ask you a question?"

Just as well. He'd only made it as far as Henry's stall—the first one by the door—before his thoughts had sneaked right back to stuff Eden loved to do for him. He swallowed. "Shoot."

"How come we don't hold hands?"

He looked up, laid his sandwich back on his plate. "Where did that come from?"

She shrugged. "I'm attracted to you. You're attracted to me. It's hard to just shut that off at midnight."

"Seems I recall being up a little later than that most nights."

"You know what I mean."

"Let me ask you a question."

Her brows arched. "I asked first. And you didn't answer."

"In a minute. How did you feel when Iris called you my wife. Be honest."

"Like we were lying to her." Her shoulders squared. "But we're not, really. They know why I'm here."

"Yeah. But you still feel guilty when we accidentally touch in public. Face it—both of us jump like scalded rabbits."

"Oh, don't be dense, Stony. That's a pure jolt of desire and you know it. We get within ten feet of each other and our hormones go haywire."

"Only ten feet for you? It's more like fifty for me."

"Then you ought to be in pretty bad shape right about now." Dimples creased her cheeks.

He was. Thank God for the table between them. "You really want to start something you can't finish here?"

"Who says I can't finish?" She reached under the table and ran her hand up the inside seam of his jeans. "There's a lock on that bathroom door over there."

Nikki skipped in with Rosie right beside her.

Stony raised his brow at Eden. "See?" And damn it all, he was hard as an oak.

She snatched her hand back and jumped up, then busily wrung out a dishrag and scrubbed at the spotlessly clean countertop.

"Hey, there, doll baby," she said brightly. "You're lookin' pert as a cricket."

Nikki fell on the floor giggling, and Stony chuckled.

"You're so silly," Nikki said.

"What? You don't think a cricket looks pert?"

Nikki glanced at Stony, then flipped up Rosie's

ear and whispered something. "Rosie wants to know what's pert mean."

"Happy," Eden supplied. "And is that all Rosie wanted to know? You two get to whispering and I worry. Y'all aren't thinking about getting into the ice cream or sugar bowl, are you?"

"Oh, no," Nikki said solemnly while shaking her head. Her eyes darted to Rosie again and she quickly changed the subject back. "We had a happy cricket in the vent by Daddy's chair and Lottie *said* it was happy 'cuz it was singin', and Daddy said somebody ought to shoot the happy out of it."

Eden and Nikki both turned accusing gazes on Stony.

"Hey, now. No need to drag me into this. I'm just sitting here eating my sandwich."

"Imagine," Eden said to no one in particular. "Threatening a cute little cricket."

"Yeah," Nikki echoed. "A *pert* one."

Thankfully, the phone rang before they could gang up on him anymore. He grabbed the portable off the table where Eden had left it.

"Stony? It's Dora. Hannah's having the baby," she said, sounding as if she was out of breath.

"Which hospital?"

"No hospital. She's delivering at home—don't ask me why. The doctor's there now—hopefully with plenty of drugs—but Ethan said I should call you, that you guys should probably go hang out with Wyatt and make sure he doesn't embarrass himself. Ethan's words, not mine."

Stony grinned. "We'll meet you there." He turned off the phone and looked up at Eden, who was practically breathing down his neck.

"Well?" she demanded

"Hannah's having the baby."

She hardly gave him a chance to get the words out. As he watched in awe, she went right into efficiency mode, loading muffins and rolls and cooking supplies into bags and boxes. She took a casserole dish from the fridge and a skillet out of the cupboard. In less than two minutes she'd snatched his half-eaten sandwich out from under him, had her purse on her shoulder, Nikki headed out the door, and a huge box shoved at his stomach.

"Here," she said. "Let's go."

He nearly saluted, but would have dropped the box she'd already let go of.

Instead he grinned. "Whatever you say, wild thing."

Chapter Twelve

Meredith Shirley Malone was born at 3:20 that afternoon. Her middle name had been chosen in honor of a beloved aunt who'd had an impact on Hannah's life and inadvertently sent her to Wyatt.

Eden was genuinely thrilled for Hannah and Wyatt and only experienced a tiny instant where her excitement warred with envy. But only for a fleeting second. Seeing how moved Wyatt was over the birth of his little girl brought tears of happiness to Eden's eyes. And the soft, profound look of love on Hannah's face was bright enough to light a forest at midnight.

God willing, Eden thought, this would be her, someday very soon.

After taking a peek and cooing over the brand-new baby, she appropriated the kitchen and effortlessly, busily worked her magic with the contents of the Malones' refrigerator, dodging children and adults every time she turned around.

Ian and Nikki were smack in the middle of the floor with laps full of puppies. Katie Callahan, just a year old and cute as a button, had tired of being told no when she'd tried to give too much love to the puppies and was now happily helping herself to the plastic ware in the lazy Susan cabinet next to the dishwasher. Ethan was watching his daughter like a hawk, and Dora, bless her heart was helping peel potatoes. She was disorganized and messy, but she got the job done.

And Stony, Eden noticed, was watching her. She knew why. He was worried about her. Her heart squeezed at the realization, and she deliberately crossed her eyes at him. He gave her one of those lazy, half smiles that made her go hot and get goose bumps at the same time.

"Good thing Hannah decided to do this at home," Dora said, oblivious that she'd just flicked a potato peel on the floor. "The hospital would never have put up with this many people underfoot at once."

Without interrupting his conversation with Stony, Ethan automatically swiped up the peel and tossed it in the sink. Eden pressed her lips together to keep from smiling, thinking theirs must have been a very interesting courtship. A messy and a neatnick.

"At least the doctor was here for her," Eden said.

"Thank goodness. I doubt that Wyatt would have held up as a midwife." Dora cut her gaze to her husband. "Amazing how these big strong guys turn to mush at the slightest little thing."

"I heard that, legs," Ethan said. "And I'll have you know that Stony's done some midwifery, and did a fine job at it."

"I was talking about babies, ace, not animals."

"So was I," Ethan said, grinning.

"Who?" Dora demanded.

"Nikki."

"Really?" Dora asked, looking at Stony.

Stony nodded. "Out on a cattle drive, at that."

"Well, my goodness. I am impressed, and I do stand corrected. *Most* big cowboys would turn to mush—with the exception of Stony." Her blue eyes twinkled when she glanced at her husband.

Ethan took a plastic lid out of Katie's mouth and said, "You're awfully sassy for a preacher's daughter."

"Comes from being a playboy's wife," she fired back.

Katie latched on to Ethan's pants, then fussed and patted her diapers. He immediately swung her up and perched her on his forearm. "Aw, sweet peach. I don't know why you can't use the toilet—never mind that you're too little and don't even talk."

Ethan kissed Katie's chubby cheek, and she gave a belly laugh that left everyone in the room smiling. "Be right back," he said, heading out of the kitchen. "Katie doesn't like admitting in front of company that she's done something unladylike in her drawers."

"See what I mean?" Dora asked. She rinsed the potato skins off her hands, dribbling water on the floor. "Turns to mush. That little girl has him wrapped around her pinky." She looked around. "Are we done here?"

Eden handed her a towel and plucked the peeler out of her hands. "Yes. Thanks for the help. Why don't you check on Hannah and Wyatt, see if they need anything."

"Good idea." She stopped on her way out of the kitchen to tickle the puppies and plant a kiss on the tops of Nikki's and Ian's heads. "You kids ought to take those animals out to the barn. Skeeter's out there, and he'll watch you.''

"'Kay,'' Ian said, and gathered two little dogs under his arms as Nikki cradled another.

Stony watched the busy activity taking place in the Malones' kitchen—and Eden was the busiest. She had a roast in the oven, biscuit dough mixed up in a bowl with a towel draped on top to keep it fresh, potatoes peeled, corn shucked, scrubbed and gently bobbing in boiling water and chocolate cake layers cooling on wire racks. Her hands moved constantly, without thought.

She was very good at this. Not only at preparing excellent-tasting meals, but organizing and adding special touches and doing it all around a roomful of people and chaos—even though she *had* glanced at Dora a time or two with amused exasperation.

He saw her hands go still for just an instant when Meredith's cries drifted downstairs. She looked around, met his gaze and smiled as though she didn't have a thing in the world on her mind.

But Stony knew her heart was alternately aching and blossoming with hope, hope that she, too, would one day hear the miraculous cry of her own child.

He moved up next to her, draped his arm across her shoulder and massaged her neck beneath the silky fall of her auburn hair.

She jerked her head toward him, obviously startled by his open display of affection, when he'd gone out of his way to avoid it before.

He'd been an idiot. Depriving them both. And he wasn't going to do it anymore. For as long as she was here, she was his.

Without a word he pressed his lips to her temple.

She sighed, put her arms around his waist and looked up at him. "I'm okay," she said.

"I know. I just had this urge to kiss that sexy blue vein just there," he said, doing it a second time.

She grinned. "Liar."

"Now when have you known me to lie?"

"Well, whether you are lying or not, I'm a greedy woman. I'll take your kisses any way I can get them."

"Maybe you two would like to get a room," Ethan suggested as he came back in, his freshly diapered daughter perched on his arm.

Eden blushed and groaned into Stony's shirtfront.

"Maybe you'd like to stuff it," Stony said back to Ethan, his smile belying his tone.

Ethan shrugged and snagged Dora when she breezed back in the kitchen. "Just trying to help out my fellow man." He bent his knees, kissed his wife. "How's it going, legs?" His voice and eyes were so filled with love it hit Stony right in the chest.

"Do that again, and I'll let you know," Dora urged.

"My pleasure," Ethan said, and kissed his wife again.

"Kind of like the pot calling the skillet black," Eden remarked to Stony. "Don't you think?"

Stony nodded just as Wyatt walked in, stopping to take in all the embracing going on in his kitchen. "You guys are doing that on purpose just to get to me," he complained.

Stony grinned, and Ethan taunted, "Six weeks, pal."

STONY RODE IN from the west pasture, where he'd been observing a stallion that had been spooked over at the Callahans' a couple months back, nearly trampling Dora and Katie. Although the proud black beauty hadn't displayed any more noticeably nasty traits, Ethan wasn't in a hurry to take the horse back, and Stony didn't push.

He swung down off Henry and saw Eden balancing baskets and dishes and putting them in the trunk of the Mustang. He handed Henry's reins to Demone. "Mind putting him away for me?"

"Sure thing."

Ian and Nikki were impersonating a couple of rabbits hopping around Eden's feet as she walked. Stony and Eden had been keeping Ian for the past two days to give Wyatt and Hannah a chance to settle, and he wondered if Wyatt had stopped grinning yet over the newest addition to their family.

Wyatt Malone was one proud man—and he had plenty of reason to be. After losing his first wife and son, Stony had begun to worry that Wyatt might never truly recover. Then Hannah had dropped into his life, a city girl with zero ranch skills and scared to death of animals, radiating a truckload of determination and a gentle spirit that had grabbed Wyatt from the first hello. You'd never know Ian and Meredith weren't his biological children.

Eden laughed at the kids' antics. "Y'all are gonna be barfin' up those pancakes if you don't settle down."

Ian stopped and stared at Eden.

"It's okay," Nikki told him. "She says stuff like that all the time. She's from *Texas*."

"Yes, ma'am, I am. Now hop yourselves in the car while I get the rest of this stuff."

Stony stepped up behind her just as she was reaching for one of the grocery sacks she'd left on the porch.

"Need some help?"

She shot straight up and pressed a hand to her bosom. "You scared the daylights out of me."

He grinned, bent down and pressed a lingering kiss to her lips. "That make it better?"

Her eyes were dazed as she licked her lips, glanced around. "Cryin' out loud."

God, he loved it when she whispered that expression in that soft drawl, her voice breathy, trembling, aroused. She had a tendency to say it after he'd done something that stunned her, annoyed her...or aroused her. It made him want to pick her up and haul her someplace private—in a hurry.

Her gaze slipped to the front of his pants then shot up to his face.

He raised his left brow. "Don't look so scandalized. You know that drawl gets to me every time."

"You better hush up and behave. The kids are right over there."

"So I see. Where are you off to?"

"Hannah called and said Wyatt's folks are coming in today, and she thought Ian should be there to meet his new grandparents."

Stony was really glad she'd just handed him a good excuse to go with her, otherwise he'd have been forced to get inventive. He'd seen her holding that little baby the other day, and he'd known it was breaking her heart. Not that she envied or begrudged Hannah and Wyatt their child. It was that she so desperately wanted her own and was so afraid to get her hopes up, knowing that there were no guarantees that her body was even capable of cooperating—of conceiving.

And he didn't want her facing that reminder alone.

"Mind if I tag along?"

She frowned. "Why?"

Because you might need me. "Because I haven't seen Wyatt's folks in a long time, and I've been itching to get my hands on the wheel of that Mustang."

Dimples winked in her cheeks when she grinned. "It is pretty racy, isn't it?" She had the key ring around her index finger and twirled it, teasing him with each jingling revolution. "But who says I should let you drive?"

"I do." He bent down and kissed her, slipped the keys off fingers that had gone slack. "Because, baby, you love it when I drive." He straightened, tossed the keys in the air and caught them, then picked up the bags off the porch and strode to the car, grinning when he made it all the way to the trunk before she came out of her daze and followed.

She went around to the passenger side, opened the door and got in, her breathing not all that steady.

"Cryin' out loud."

Stony laughed, pulled her seat belt across her shoulder, because she seemed to have forgotten, and reversed out of the driveway.

By the time they reached the turnoff to the Malones', Eden had herself under control. Stony Stratton could kiss the socks off a rooster, that was for sure. And it was absolutely pitiful how she went completely stupid every time he turned on that charm.

She'd wanted him to let their relationship out of the bedroom, but decided she just might have made a huge tactical error. Becoming mindless in the middle of the night was one thing—going through the daylight hours in a stupor would never do.

She tugged at her snug, cotton top. Either she was going to have to learn a little more control or buy some padded bras. Because the flimsy one she was wearing didn't hide a darn thing. And it was embarrassing to parade around in public looking as if her bosoms had been caught in a deep freeze—especially when the sun was shining and the temperatures hovered around eighty.

"You doing okay over there, wild thing?"

She barely waited for him to shut off the engine before she opened the door and got out of the car. Pointing a finger at him she said, "You just keep your distance."

He grinned. "Now she changes her tune."

"Sugar, my tune's singin' so loud one of us is going to end up red in the face. And since I figure that someone's going to be me, I'd appreciate you turning down the wattage just a hair."

Nikki and Ian bounded out of the car and took off toward the barn as three dogs raced toward them.

"Halt," Eden said.

Kids and dogs alike skidded to a stop. Surprised, Eden glanced at Stony and raised her brows. "That was fairly impressive, don't you think?"

His lips twitched.

She looked back at the kids. "Y'all have ten minutes. Then I want you to come inside and be sociable. And don't be bringing the puppies and kittens in the house. Meredith needs time to get used to breathin' in this world before she has to snort animal fur.''

"'Kay,'' Ian said, and Nikki nodded, both kids poised like sprinters waiting for the starting gunshot at a race.

Eden waved her hand. ''Go.'' She grabbed a wicker basket from the trunk. ''I hope Hannah's feelings don't get hurt that Ian was more interested in playing in the barn than speaking to her after being gone two days.''

''I think she'll survive.''

Eden gave a cursory knock on the back door, then went on in. No sense making somebody get up needlessly just to open a door.

Hannah was at the kitchen table nursing the baby. She had the receiving blanket over her shoulder, nicely preserving her modesty, and didn't appear to be the least bit self-conscious.

Still, Eden stopped abruptly, causing Stony to plow into her, nearly sending her sprawling headfirst into the kitchen. She managed to set down the basket she carried, and Stony managed to keep her upright...and with her dignity intact.

His strength and size continually surprised her. He could lift her with one hand, as though she weighed no more than Nikki. And he did it a lot. And every single time he did it she felt cherished...and so aroused she could hardly see straight.

Turning, she relieved him of the sacks he held, putting them on the floor just inside the door. ''Shoo. Go talk to Wyatt about some cows or something, so Hannah can have some privacy.''

When she straightened and met his eyes, she went very still. He was watching her, carefully, steadily, gauging her emotions. The sensual teasing they'd been toying with minutes ago had softened the look in his whiskey gaze into something incredibly moving.

She knew that look. It was the one he wore when he held her in his lap, brushing away her tears, the one he wore when he brought her pain medication and rubbed her temples until she fell asleep, the one that still remained when she woke up less than an hour later and raced to the bathroom.

It was a look that said his arms and his strength were there for her, that he wouldn't let her fall, that he would catch her just as he had seconds ago when she'd lost her balance, that if it was within his power, he'd make all her wrongs right.

He was worried about her. Worried that she'd be sad.

Eden laid her palm along the side of his face and said quietly, "I know what you're doing." *And I love you for it.*

The emotion literally jolted her. She scrambled to cover it by closing her eyes and giving him a quick, friendly kiss. "Now, git."

This man saw way too much.

FALL HAD BARELY BEEN in the air before the snow came, and Eden was learning right quick that she didn't know squat about driving in the icy stuff.

With clammy, white-knuckled hands, she gripped the steering wheel of the Mustang, her face practically pressed to the cold plastic as she negotiated the slippery highway, driving as slow as a snail. The heater blew full blast, but she still shivered.

Jim and Mary Malone had left Shotgun Ridge,

insisting that Wyatt and Hannah didn't need house guests—never mind that the house was partly theirs. They'd found after years of ranch life that they both had a touch of wanderlust and were enjoying traveling the country and wintering in warmer climates. They promised to be back by Christmas and schedule regular visits with their grandchildren.

And Eden had been cooking up a storm ever since, delivering extras to all the neighbors.

Her period had come in September.

And again in October.

She tried to tell herself there was no correlation between that and her grocery bill—the bill that she and Stony were continually butting heads over.

The strain was starting to take its toll. Eden was edgy and so was Stony. He still reached for her several times each night, but Eden was beginning to worry that he was doing it out of a sense of duty. Oh, he still turned her mindless with his expert touch, but sometimes she got the feeling he was holding back, that it was all for her, just a desperate attempt to connect his sperm to her egg.

Coming up on a curve, she lightly touched the brakes and felt the sporty car slip on a patch of ice. Adrenaline shot the blood straight to her head, making her see stars.

She made a distressed little sound in the back of her throat and tried not to panic. She'd learned that on icy roads the driver had very little to do with which direction the car was going. Regardless of brake pedals and steering wheels—equipment designed expressly to put the driver in control—it slid willy-nilly at the slightest provocation and there wasn't a blessed thing she could do about it.

It scared the living daylights out of her, reminded her of those simulators in driver's ed. Or those video games where the race car was zooming around the track, but the steering wheel didn't work without putting money in the slot. It was a weird feeling to turn the wheel to the right, expecting to go that way, only to have the silly vehicle keep right on going straight—or sideways as it had done coming out of town. It was a wonder she hadn't ended up in the ditch.

Embarrassing, demoralizing and thoroughly nerve-racking.

Honestly, what was the point of bragging that the snowplow had scraped the streets if it didn't do any better job than this.

The back end of the car finally quit doing the snake, and the tires found purchase on the asphalt once more. *Thank you, Lord.*

Eden took her hand off the wheel long enough to wipe her sweaty palm on her jeans. All around, she had to admit it'd been a bad day to go shopping.

And thank goodness Nikki was spending the weekend at Dora and Ethan's, helping out with Katie and playing with the menagerie of animals Dora seemed to collect. Otherwise she might have been right here beside Eden, risking life and limb on these gawd-awful, slip-and-slide roads.

When the ranch came into sight, Eden wanted to get out and hug the fence. How in the world would anybody run a catering service in this town when the weather and roads weren't user-friendly? She threaded the car between the poles of the arched Triple S sign, but evidently got a little too big for her britches when she attempted to negotiate the circular driveway. She missed it completely, and there she went, heading for the barn.

Uh-oh, she thought as the tail end of the car switched places with the front. On the way around, she'd gotten a glimpse of Stony's astonished face. He was just stepping into a beefy-looking truck with monster tires, and she wasn't sure if he was arriving or about to depart.

By the time the back end of the car had put itself nicely in the doorway of the barn, Stony was wrenching her door open.

And he was madder than a red ant.

"What in the hell is the matter with you?" His hands were on his hips now. Demone and Marcus discreetly disappeared.

Frigid air, fragrant with wood smoke, bit at her cheeks and went right down the collar of her pitifully inadequate coat—which is why she'd even braved the nightmare-causing roads in the first place.

Reluctantly she swung her legs out of the car. A gentleman even through the obvious haze of pique, he cupped her elbows and brought her to her feet, holding on just long enough to make sure she was steady. She doubted he even realized he'd done it.

She flexed her fingers to get the circulation moving again and blew into her palms, but before she could form an appropriate answer to his question of her sanity, he cut loose.

"What the hell possessed you to take this piss ant car out without a decent set of snow tires? My God, have you ever even *driven* in the snow? And where are your gloves?" He snatched her hands, cradled them between his big, warm palms.

The impatience coupled with gentleness stopped

her for a moment. A big guy, hopping mad—yet clearly, without thought, he was automatically, innately gentle. Amazing.

However, she'd had a harrowing afternoon and didn't intend to sit still for a dressing down. She lifted her gaze from their hands to his eyes.

"First, I didn't realize the *piss ant* car needed decent tires, since the ones on it have barely got ten thousand miles on them, and no, I wasn't trying to kill myself or anyone else, and I don't think anyone actually *drives* in the snow since the vehicle seems to insist on doing that all by itself." She took a breath. "Aside from *that* firsthand observation—no, I've *never* driven in the snow, my nerves are shot, and my gloves are in a King's Western Wear shopping bag in the trunk—which is apparently warming itself in your barn."

He stared at her for a full five seconds. Then he gripped her arms, hauled her flush against his chest, practically lifting her off her toes, and kissed her hard.

For a moment Eden was too stunned to react. Then she understood where all the aggression came from.

By dog, he cared.

She reached between them, slipped her hand inside his heavy coat and rubbed gently right over his heart.

His lips immediately softened. After a minute he let her feet rest fully on the ground and leaned his forehead against hers.

"You scared me," he said quietly.

"I know. I'm sorry. But I was really cold. Texas

winters aren't like this, and none of my clothes were heavy enough.''

''Why didn't you wait for me to get back?''

''I wasn't sure when that would be. And since Nikki's with Dora, I figured this was the best time to go.''

''You should have taken one of the trucks.''

She shook her head. ''I've never driven your truck, and I thought I'd feel more comfortable taking the car since I'm used to how it handles.'' She shuddered. ''Bad choice. A time or two I was certain I'd ended up on the teacup ride at Six Flags over Texas.''

The side of his mouth turned up. He shook his head and kissed her forehead. ''I'm sorry I yelled.''

''Technically, you never raised your voice.''

He gave her an indulgent look, then opened his coat and pulled her inside, shoving the panels of her thin wool coat out of the way so she could benefit from the fiery warmth of his chest.

Eden had been cold for so long, she decided she might just stay right here for the rest of the winter— *fall* and winter, she amended. Who ever heard of snow before trick-or-treating?

She breathed in the crisp smell of bracing air and leather that clung to Stony's skin, beginning to feel somewhat steadier.

''Wyatt's first wife and their baby boy died in a car accident,'' he said quietly. ''I don't know why that took hold in my mind when I saw your car gone, but it did.''

She tightened her arms around his waist, apologized and soothed with the sketch of her hands over his back. She wasn't sure when soothing turned into more. Her heart began to thump when she felt him growing hard against her, felt the pressure of his palm increase at the small of her back, drawing her in. She sucked in a breath, shifted slightly and rubbed against him, torturing herself.

The conversation she'd had with Carrie played through her mind, and she smiled against his shirt-front. *Jeans molded so perfectly you can* see *which side of his fly...*

And feel it, she thought.

"Do you need any of those shopping bags right away?"

Oh, my gosh. She knew that deep, seductive tone. It nearly shouted that he was going to take her in the house and turn her inside out.

Her heart lodged in her mouth, and she had a little trouble getting her tongue unstuck from the roof of her mouth. Nikki wasn't home, and Eden saw by the flare in Stony's eyes that he'd just recalled that liberating bit of information.

They hadn't made love during the day since the first weekend of their marriage, and just recalling it made her go weak.

"Depends," she finally said. "I *am* kind of cold and there's a cozy pair of long johns in one of those sacks."

He bent at the knees, tightened his arm around her waist, and when he straightened, their faces were level and her feet were nearly a foot off the ground.

"Baby, when I get through with you, you'll be pitching those long johns and begging me to turn on the air-conditioning."

Chapter Thirteen

Stony parked his truck behind the veterinarian's office, even though he was going next door to the medical clinic. He didn't want half the town speculating as to why Stony Stratton was visiting the doctor.

Well, Stony Stratton was getting a little worried about his virility, that's why. It had been four months, and Eden still wasn't pregnant. And though he was more embarrassed than he could ever remember being, this discussion with the doctor was something he had to have.

Still, he didn't want the whole town to know, and since Chance had told him he'd hired a new nurse—one of the women who'd come for the town's bachelor auction and stayed—Stony was a little unsure if she upheld the rules of confidentiality. He had no idea who the woman was or if she'd end up letting something slip.

He punched numbers into his cell phone, and after barely a minute the nurse put him through to the doctor.

"Stony," Chance said. "What can I do for you?"

"I need an appointment, but I'd just as soon no one know I'm here."

"What do you mean, here? Where are you?"

"Behind the clinic. Parked in back of the vet's office." Stony had always thought it odd that the doc and the vet had set up shop right next door to each other. Hell of a thing if someone got confused and went in the wrong door.

"I take it you're not anxious to run into my nurse, too?"

"Yeah." He sighed. "It's important, Chance."

"Okay. Give me five minutes. I'll send Grace over to Brewer's for an early lunch. We don't have any patients scheduled until this afternoon, anyway. Come through the back door."

Stony was sweating and nauseous by the time he got out of the truck and let himself in the back door of the clinic.

Chance Hammond, wearing a white lab coat over jeans and T-shirt, closed the door to his office and sat behind his desk. "So, what can I do for you?"

Stony studied the doctor for a moment. Chance wasn't slouched in the chair waiting like a ghoul for an opportunity to tease as they normally did. As friends did. And neither was his body rigid as if he was dreading a question that might make them both uncomfortable. His posture was relaxed and professional.

"Eden's not pregnant yet. It's been four months."

Chance gave a slight nod. "Nature's fickle, Stony, and Eden's body is weak." His eye contact was direct, regretful. "It might not happen."

"Maybe not. But since I've never actually fa-

thered a child, I'd like to be sure it's not me who
can't make it happen.''

''I doubt that's the case, but I can certainly run a
test.''

Stony felt some of the stiffness drain out of his
shoulders. Just like that, Chance had known what to
say.

Stony nodded. There wasn't any time to waste.
Because if it turned out that the problem was him,
that he couldn't father a child, Eden would need
time to find someone else. The thought made him
want to put his fist through the nearest wall, but he
knew he would release her in a minute. No woman
deserved to go through the debilitating anemia Eden
was suffering. Surgery would correct it, but that
would break her heart. She deserved every chance
at a successful conception that he could give her.

''Yeah, I'd like to do the test.''

BY THE THIRD WEEK IN NOVEMBER Eden could no
longer suppress the giddiness, the nausea…and the
fear.

Her period was late.

She pressed her hand to her abdomen. Was there
even now the tiny beginnings of a baby in her
womb?

Or what if the absence of heavy flow was some
freaky phase of the disease that Dr. Amies might
have mentioned but Eden hadn't remembered? She
wondered if a person could wish away their men-
strual cycle. One of her employees had missed two
months due to stress and, Eden suspected, nearly
starving herself to death. An anorexic working at a
catering company. Hard to imagine, but that's how

it had turned out. Thankfully Jennifer had gotten help and was on the mend.

Eden went into the downstairs bathroom, opened the drawer where a couple of pregnancy test boxes lay. She'd bought two, figuring if she only got one, fate might slap her down for being overconfident. Plus, if she had to go back to the store more than once, that'd be like taking out an ad in the paper that Eden Williams—Stratton, she amended with a little tickle in her stomach—wasn't pregnant.

She touched the box, her hands trembling. One pink line for no. Two pink lines for yes.

She slammed the drawer shut and leaned against the counter, pressed her hands prayer-like to her lips. *Don't count your chickens before they hatch. Don't jinx it.*

She stood there debating for a good ten minutes, then finally addressed her reflection in the mirror. "This is ridiculous, Eden. It's just a little box. It's not a snake. If it says no, you'll deal with it." She plowed her fingers through her hair, closed her fists, felt the pull against her scalp. "Okay. If I don't get my period by tonight, I'll do it."

She snatched open the bathroom door and plowed right into Stony's chest. "Oh!"

He steadied her with his hands at her elbows, his expression concerned, searching. He knew when her period was due, and from that very first embarrassing time after the Fourth of July, he'd made a habit of watching her closely around the second week of the month, agonizing with her, taking care of her when pain and weakness made it difficult to stay on her feet.

This wasn't the first time she'd found him outside

the bathroom door, waiting, ready to catch her if she crumbled.

His thumb swept softly across her cheek. "You're still late, aren't you?"

She could feel her lips tremble when she smiled, feel the giddy host of butterflies in her stomach, feel her heart jumping. "Yes."

"Did you take the test?"

Now her hands were trembling. "I was going to wait till tonight."

He raised his brows.

"I'm scared," she whispered.

"Then don't do it."

She shook her head. "It'll drive me nuts. I have to know one way or the other." Drawing air into her lungs, hoping to calm some of these nerves, she decided that it was now or never. It was pure foolishness to act this way. "Okay. Go away." If he waited outside the door, she probably wouldn't be able to pee. She whirled and went back in the bathroom, ripped the cellophane off the box and read the instructions three more times.

Stony made a pot of coffee to give himself something to do. He couldn't believe how uptight he was, the expectation. The thought of his baby growing inside Eden excited him, and it worried him.

He whirled around when she came out of the bathroom, and he knew it wasn't good news even before she shook her head. He couldn't remember ever seeing such a desolate expression on a person's face. Her eyes were dry, as though the hurt went too deep for tears.

He stepped toward her, but she held up her hand. "Don't."

Stony thought his heart was going to rip open and bleed. That single word held so much pain the sound practically stung. "Eden—"

"I'm fine." Her tone was abrupt, her hand still up to keep him from closing the distance between them. "I mean it, Stony. Don't touch me…please. I…I just need some time. Because if you're nice to me right now I think I might shatter."

She left the room, and Stony felt his throat ache. Her sorrow scraped him raw.

Nikki came bursting in the back door. "Where's Eden? Can she come watch me ride Pony?"

"Not just now, Nik. She's not feeling good. How about if I come, though."

"Okay. But I gotta go potty first."

Stony waited for Nikki to come back out, wishing he knew what to say to Eden. Chance had put a rush on the lab test and had called to tell him everything checked out A-okay.

The relief had been so strong, he'd had to sit down.

So, damn it, why couldn't that pregnancy test have been positive?

By the time Nikki finished doing her business in the bathroom, she'd decided against riding the pony and took off to play hide-and-seek with Rosie.

Stony went out to the barn, vacating the kitchen so that if Eden wanted to come back in and work out her emotions in a bowlful of bread dough, she'd have the solitude to do so.

But by dinner the strain was about to eat Stony alive. She was so quiet. He knew she was hurting, and he couldn't do a damned thing about it.

As soon as she put Nikki to bed, Eden went into

their bedroom and shut the door. Stony paced in front of the fireplace for ten minutes, then decided he couldn't keep this up. He gentled horses every day, never crowded them, waited patiently until they were ready to come to him. And when he turned his back, he was telling the horse he trusted him, his body language asking the horse to trust him, too.

That's what Eden was doing to him, he decided. Turning away because she trusted him. And that meant he could follow.

And if it didn't? Well, that was just too damned bad. He took the stairs two at a time. She wasn't going to be alone with her sadness one more minute.

His heart thumped in his chest as he opened the door, saw her standing by the window gazing out at the stars, arms wrapped around her waist hugging herself. He strode across the room, caught her just as she turned, lifted her right up against him and covered her mouth with his before she had a chance to put up a shield. He poured every ounce of his frustration, desire, sorrow and his soul into that kiss.

When she made a little sound of surrender and wound her arms around his neck he nearly shook. He'd wanted to chase away her shadows, and she'd just joined in the race, her mouth eating at his, her arms squeezing, her breasts flattened against his chest. There was frenzy in her actions, and in his, their mouths dueling as though they were mortal enemies one minute, thrusting and parrying, then wild lovers the next, unable to get close enough, wanting in, seeking to appease and be appeased.

He tasted the salt of her tears and pulled back, looking down at her. The rivulets spilling from the corners of her eyes and down her cheeks stung his heart like drops of acid.

"Oh, baby, don't." He held her tighter than he meant to, pressed her head to his shoulder. He needed her like mad, but he had to get a rein on his emotions. She was fragile, and he was tied in knots. The last thing in the world he wanted to do was hurt her more.

She resisted his efforts to cradle her. With hands that trembled, she framed his face, looked deep into eyes, let him see the sadness there, the invitation, the plea.

"Are you sure?" His voice was barely above a whisper, feeling as if it had scraped all the way up his throat.

She nodded, pressed her lips against his neck. "Don't be gentle with me, Stony. I need…"

"I know what you need, baby. We'll stop the clock, even if it's just for tonight." And he wished like hell the clock *would* stop. Because only thirty-nine days remained before their six months were up—and that wasn't enough.

A COUPLE OF DAYS LATER Eden began spotting. She popped more vitamin and iron tablets, waiting for the inevitable blood loss, the debilitating tiredness. She didn't need this now. She had twenty or so people coming for Thanksgiving dinner. When the rush of blood didn't come, Eden took it as a blessing. Maybe…just maybe the disease was going into remission. Oh, if only…

She baked pies and corn bread, mixed up dough for rolls and sautéed celery and onions, filling the house with warmth and mouthwatering scents.

When the turkey was cleaned and dressed and in the oven, she set the dining-room table for eighteen and draped a washable tablecloth over a folding table for the kids. Even though they were only expecting about twenty guests, there was seating here for at least twenty-five. One thing she'd say about these Montana ranches—they had banquet-size dining rooms—at least the three she'd been in did.

Floor-to-ceiling French windows let in light and offered the postcard view of pristine snow piled atop fences and pillowed over barn roofs. A fire crackled in the corner fireplace, the flames casting dancing shadows over the cherry wood floors. The high ceiling, too, was covered in wood, intricately carved, with deep crown molding around the perimeter. A built-in hutch, marble-topped sideboard and Chippendale table were also stained in various hues of cherry, the chair cushions covered in crushed blue velvet. The warmth of wood and china and velvet invited you to come in and sit a spell and be part of the family.

With an apron tied over her wool sweater and slacks, and ribbons decorating her hair, Eden breezed back into the kitchen and had the potatoes boiling when the guests began to arrive.

From there the house filled with laughter, teasing, children running and shrieking, dogs scrambling and general chaos. Eden dodged it all, in her element. The sheriff, Cheyenne Bodine, came in his squad car with Chance Hammond riding shotgun, which garnered the poor doctor plenty of teasing. Ethan and his brothers Grant and Clay were in the den along with Wyatt, Stony and the old cronies, all of them arguing over something Eden couldn't hear.

Dora breezed in, and Eden prayed she wouldn't offer to help. Hannah, sitting at the kitchen table nursing the baby, met Eden's eyes and smiled. Obviously she knew Dora's disorganization, too. Vera and Iris were busy arranging olives, onions and cranberry sauce in cut-glass condiment dishes.

"Naturally they're in there fighting over the remote," Dora said, snitching an olive off the dish as soon as Iris set it down. "Switching back and forth between the ball game and car racing. What is it with men and gadgets. It's a wonder Ethan and his brothers don't kill each other over who gets to *hold* the thing." As quickly as she'd whirled in the kitchen, Dora whirled out again.

The next thing Eden knew, Ethan was shouting. She ran into the den, heart pounding, worried sick someone had been hurt—Katie? Nikki? Ian?

Hannah, Vera and Iris followed.

Ethan had Dora in his lap, holding her as though she was about to expire before his eyes. "Easy, legs." He looked terrified. "Chance, get the hell over here."

"Language, Ethan," Clay and Grant admonished.

"For Pete's sake, Ethan," Dora said.

"Hush up." He ignored his brothers and glared at Chance who was squatting in front of them, looking at Dora with an enigmatic smile on his face.

"She nearly fainted," Ethan said. "By God, she'd have fallen on the floor if I hadn't been there. What's the matter with her? Sweetheart, let Chance have a look at you."

"If you'd let one of us get a word in edgewise, I'd tell you that I'm not sick."

"Yes you are. You lost every bit of your color

and nearly fainted dead away. I saw you with my own—''

''I'm pregnant.''

''—eyes, and if you'd quit being so stubborn and…'' He snapped his mouth shut, stared at her dumbfounded. ''What did you say? Did you say…?'' He swallowed hard. ''You're…?'' a whisper now.

She nodded, smiled softly at him. ''Going to have your baby.''

As Ethan kissed his wife with a tenderness that touched every person in the room, Ozzie Peyton said softly, ''That is fine, fine news, you bet. Just what we planned for. Isn't that right, boys?'' Henry, Lloyd and Vern all nodded.

Eden's emotions were riding as high as everyone else's in the room. The love and happiness between Dora and Ethan Callahan was so utterly tangible, it was as though each person here had somehow shared a part in the pregnancy.

The image of her own pregnancy test with a single pink line flashed in Eden's mind, but the wound of disappointment wasn't raw and bleeding any longer. Stony had made sure of that.

She looked across the room, didn't see him, then felt his hand at her neck, under her hair. He tucked her against his side, his palm spanning the entire width of her back as he rubbed from the top of her spine to the bottom and back again.

She noticed how the others around them darted quick, concerned glances at her. Just that, though. They didn't fuss. The support and love in this room was overwhelming.

She'd expected to form friendships when she'd

come to Montana, but nothing like this. Nothing so genuine. My gosh, even a trip to the market meant you'd better just mark off the whole day because you would run into so many people to chat with you'd think you were at a reunion.

In the city Eden couldn't tell for sure if a clerk was new or had been there for forty years—and being in the food business, Eden spent a lot of time at the market. She thought about the business she'd built from scratch, sacrificed for—even putting on hold the pursuit of a relationship, husband and children.

Garden of Eden had ten employees now, and they'd moved the operation out of Eden's kitchen and into a five-thousand-square-foot building equipped with industrial-size ovens, built-in appliances, freezers, gadgets and anything else a chef could wish for. She'd mortgaged her house to the hilt and paid the loan off within a year.

Here in Shotgun Ridge, Eden was still doing what she loved, cooking for others—just not for profit. Unless someone asked for something special, like Iris introducing a more extensive dessert menu at Brewer's. Eden didn't mind running the orders into town, now that she'd gotten the hang of driving Stony's big ol' truck with the huge knobby tires. She felt like king of the hill—or highway rather.

And why in the world was she comparing Montana to her own home in the first place?

"Now I've really done it," Ethan said with an exuberant laugh. "I got the preacher's daughter pregnant."

Eden squeezed Stony's waist, then slipped from

beneath his arm and went to Dora, hugging her friend tight. "I'm so tickled for you."

"Oh, Eden. I wasn't going to announce this to-night—"

"Nonsense. This is the perfect time. You're surrounded by friends and family." She grinned. "And just think, you won't have to worry about the grapevine getting the facts all distorted. Bless it, by the time the news got all the way down the line they'd have had you adopting a monkey instead of having a baby."

Dora laughed, squeezed Eden tight. "Love does strange and wonderful things, Eden. You keep hold of that thought, and everything else will work itself out."

IN BED THAT NIGHT, after the kitchen was clean and the guests were gone, when Stony's body was buried deep inside hers, Dora's words came back to Eden.

Love does strange and wonderful things.

Oh, yes, Eden thought. The touch of his hands, the press of his lips, the light in his gaze all told her Stony cared about her. That this was much more than just fulfilling a promise. Could anyone be this gentle otherwise? Could the chemistry be this strong? Was it just compassion, or was it more? She wanted to ask but didn't have the courage.

Suddenly she felt urgency sweep through her, fear battering at the edges of her vision, a sense of foreboding she didn't understand. What would she do if she lost him? If there wasn't more? She started to move beneath him, felt as though crucial moments would slip through her fingers if she didn't hurry, show him, pour her heart out.

"Shh," he whispered as though he'd heard her thoughts. He held her still, pressed harder, deeper inside her. And that's it.

He didn't move, yet she could feel the clutch of pleasure begin, felt her body involuntarily squeeze him, saw his eyes close and a muscle in his jaw flinch. He shifted higher, gave one slow, deep thrust, and with nothing more than the steady pressure of his body filling hers, Eden crested the peak of bliss. Her fingers bit into his buttocks, pulling him tighter. Holding him motionless, deeper, harder, she undulated her hips beneath him, against him.

Violent spasms contracted over and over, seemed to have no end, the glove-tight squeezing of her feminine muscles bringing Stony right along with her. With his lips pressed to hers, his palms cradling her head, he emptied his seed into her, kissed her as though she were the most cherished gift he could ask for, gazed at her so tenderly she could have wept.

There *was* more.

"I love you," she whispered.

Chapter Fourteen

Eden was about to wear a hole in the kitchen floor, pacing, debating. Two weeks ago she'd told Stony she loved him. But he hadn't said it back. He'd just tucked her against his side, held her as though he did.

Eden hoped like crazy she wasn't fixing to make a big mistake. She picked up the portable phone, stood by the sink where snow piled on the outside windowsill and heat from apple pies in the oven and hot spiced cider bubbling on the stove fogged the glass.

"Hey there, partner," she said when Carrie answered. "You sound harried. Christmas season getting to you? Only ten shopping days left, you know."

"Hush your mouth. I've barely started, and the kids want everything they see on every commercial. About the time I think Santa's got his list checked twice, the dang thing changes! How about you? As organized as you usually are? Bring me up to date."

Eden laughed. "I know something about want lists changing daily. Nikki insists Rosie—a black Irish setter, by the way—is thinkin' up the stuff.

And I'm not quite as organized this year. The snow makes shopping a bit of a challenge. It's freezing here, Carrie. And driving icy roads is a lesson in humility, though I'm proud to say I've only dented the bumper on the truck twice.''

"Just the bumper?" Carrie asked.

"Well, the fender got a little crease in it, but that wasn't my fault. It was a woman with a runaway shopping cart—thing just pulled her right along like she was waterskiing on ice. I got so tickled, and then I felt really bad when the cart bounced off the fender and she went sprawling.''

Carrie laughed. "Dang, I miss you, Will.''

"So come see me. Mama and Daddy are coming in this afternoon. And Shotgun Ridge is so beautiful, Carrie, with Christmas lights and holly and snowmen wearing all manner of festive garments. It's all white and sparkly—''

"And cold," Carrie said.

"Yes, but the smell of wood smoke from all the chimneys is so wonderful, and it just makes you feel warmer somehow.''

"It does sound tempting, but we're crazy-busy here. I've hired two more people and dragged John and the kids in to help. You should see them, Eden. Crystal and Steven look so cute in tuxedos—if John's with me, we take the kids rather than trying to find a last-minute sitter. They love it and they're really a big help. And if I play my cards right, I might be able to sweet-talk John into quitting the factory and coming to work with me.''

Eden felt a little zing pierce her chest at the realization that she truly was expendable. She shook her head. This was Carrie. Her lifelong friend. And it gave Eden's heart a lift that Carrie was excited and thriving and had such dedication and love for the business Eden had started out of her own kitchen ten years ago, having to literally drag Carrie into it as a partner.

"Well, I guess you don't need me, then."

"Don't be silly," Carrie said quickly. "I didn't mean—"

"I know, Mugs."

AFTER SHE GOT OFF THE PHONE with Carrie, Eden sat Nikki at the table with a glass of milk and plate of Christmas cookies.

"You sit right there, sugar. I'll be back quick as a wink. And when the judge gets here, we'll dump flour all over the table and have us a Christmas cookie cutting party."

"Can Rosie help?"

Eden grinned. "I'll see if I can find a job for her."

She went into the bathroom off the kitchen, opened the drawer on the left, took out the pregnancy test box, ripped the cellophane off and tossed the instructions in the trash. She wasn't going to be a ninny about the whole process this time. If she was pregnant, she was pregnant. If she wasn't, she'd make an appointment and haul herself down to Dr. Hammond's and find out what the problem was. She wasn't going to fall apart. She wasn't going to get her hopes up. She wasn't going to—

Glass shattering against granite and Nikki's bloodcurdling scream brought Eden right up off the toilet before she'd finished peeing on the test strip. She slung the stick on the counter, yanking up her stretch pants as she ran into the kitchen, her heart in her mouth, fear nearly blinding her.

Nikki was sitting stock-still on top of the counter, glass slivered around her knees and on the floor, screaming her lungs out.

"Rosie, stay," Eden commanded as she raced across the room, lifted Nikki out of harm's way and hugged her tight.

"What in the world? Shh. Shh. You're okay." She could hardly draw in a full breath as panic ran amok through her system. Nikki was crying as though she was mortally wounded, but Eden hadn't seen any blood.

With her legs clinging like a monkey's around Eden's waist, Nikki continued to sob.

"There, doll baby. It's all right. I've got you now. Rosie, come here. We don't need you cutting your paws."

Eden sat at the kitchen table with Nikki in her lap, her little legs and arms still wrapped tight. Her heart still hadn't settled, and she considered cutting loose and squalling right along with her little girl. "Hush now, and tell me where you're hurt, sugar."

Nikki sucked in a breath, leaned back and held up her index finger as though she was E.T. Eden's eyes nearly crossed trying to see so close. "Cryin' out loud. All that caterwauling over that little bitty ol' scratch?"

"It stings," Nikki said. Amazingly enough, she'd turned off the waterworks as quickly as they'd begun.

"I think you scared yourself is what you did. Scared me right off the pot."

Nikki giggled.

"So what happened?"

"Rosie wanted a glass of milk with her cookies, too."

"Sugar, wait for me next time and I'll help. Okay?"

"Okay." Nikki wiggled her finger. "It still hurts."

"I bet a Snoopy bandage would fix it right up. Do you know where they are?" Nikki nodded, perking up. So did Rosie. The two together were a menace. "Okay, hop down and get the bandage while I get this glass picked up."

A few minutes later Eden dumped glass in the trash can, then lifted Nikki to her lap and wrapped the bandage around her tiny little finger and pressed it to her lips. "There. I kissed it and made it all better."

Nikki twisted in Eden's lap and plastered herself like taffy to Eden's chest. "I love you to pieces."

Oh, my gosh. Eden's heart leaped right into her throat. "Oh, doll baby, I love you, too." And she did. Now if she could just get Nikki's daddy to fall in line all would be well.

Except— Oh, Lord, she'd forgotten all about the test!

"Can Rosie and me go play Barbies till the judge gets here and we get to make the cookies?"

Nikki had a look in her eyes that made Eden suspicious. "Y'all aren't gonna play in the fireplace or anything?"

Nikki giggled and shook her head back and forth with enough force to give herself whiplash.

"Here, now, you're gonna get dizzy as a doodle bug." She set Nikki on the floor. "Scoot. Your daddy'll be back from the airport with my parents in just a bit.''

When Nikki and Rosie bounded up the stairs, Eden made herself walk into the bathroom. Bravely. As though she didn't care one way or the other.

''Okay, where the heck did it go?'' It wasn't on the counter. She looked on the floor, got on her knees and checked behind the commode. She was starting to feel sick at her stomach with all this fear zinging around. First Nikki, and now the blasted stick had disappeared. Maybe it was an omen. God didn't want her to find it, if it was bad news. She scooted the trash can out of the way—and there it was. She must have flung it so hard it had slid right across the vanity top and kept on going.

She held her breath, felt her stomach flip, felt like a thousand wasps were stinging from the base of her sternum clear up to her throat.

Only one pink stripe.

She swallowed, bit her bottom lip. ''Okay, Eden, deal with it. If it was meant to be, it'd be. And starin' at the blessed thing isn't going to make it grow another stripe.'' She tossed it in the trash, opened the bathroom door and came face-to-face with the kitchen door opening, Stony and her parents shaking snow off their hats and coats.

Stony glanced up at her. His gaze went from the bathroom and back. All within an instant his eyes widened in question, lit with excitement, then settled softly into *Oh, baby, I'm sorry*.

Eden smiled to let him know she wasn't about to start bawling, then looked at her mother. And then she almost *did* start bawling. Beverley Williams opened her arms, and Eden stepped into them and swallowed hard. Darn it, she was not going to fall apart in her mama's arms. And somehow Beverley understood.

"I know, darlin'," she whispered, her alto voice shaking a bit. "And I imagine you've done enough crying these past months, so we'll not do anymore today, hmm?"

Eden gave a watery chuckle and kissed her mother's cheek. "I've missed you, Mama."

"Yes, I'm quite sure you've had a time of it without my meddling in your affairs and your daddy tryin' to tell you how to cook."

Eden grinned. "Well, I have to admit you are pretty good at settling people's lives when you're all decked out in your judge's robes, and Daddy does know his way around the kitchen. I could be worse off." She turned. "Hey, Daddy," she said softly and hugged him tight. "Y'all get in here out of the cold. Are your suitcases still in the truck?"

She looked at Stony, but he merely shrugged. "I'm just the driver."

"We're staying at that charming boarding house in town, darlin'," Beverley said. "Didn't I tell you? Now don't fuss. We've already checked in, and Mildred and Opal are truly hospitable. And your daddy's already struck a bargain with the lovely couple at Brewer's Saloon and plans to cook up a storm while he's here."

"My gosh. You certainly got acquainted and acclimated in a hurry."

"We had an advantage. Lottie brought pictures and plenty of stories. We feel like folks here are old friends."

"Did you bring Aunt Lottie?"

"No. She and Ray went on to Florida. Evidently your neighbors, the Malones, have people staying down there."

"Wyatt's parents."

"That's it." Beverley took off her gloves and coat. "Now, let's get us introduced to the little sunshine in this household—and her cohort, Rosie, an intelligent Irish setter if I'm to understand correctly."

Eden grinned. Just like the judge to get all the facts beforehand.

THE FOLLOWING DAY Eden's heart leaped into her throat again, and adrenaline sent fire ants over her skin, making her feel faint.

Demone was coming up to the back door, Stony's arm slung around his shoulder. The man, two times older and two times smaller was practically carrying her husband.

Eden snatched open the door. "What happened?" She could hardly get her breath. Panic zinged, and she tried to control it.

"Devil horse kicked him right in the family jewels."

Automatic reflex had Eden reaching out to touch. It was instinctive. Stony scowled at her, and she jerked her hand back.

"Doc's coming," Demone said. "I called him from the barn half an hour ago."

"Half an hour? Where have y'all been?"

"Took a good while for Stony to get his legs under him."

"There's not a damned thing wrong with my vocal cords, and I'd appreciate the two of you not talking around me as though I'm an oak planted in the middle of the floor.''

Eden's gaze darted down, then up again. She knew this wasn't a laughing matter, but she still had the urge to do so. And he did look a bit like an oak—a terribly upset one—towering over her and Demone the way he was. She swallowed the inappropriate bubble of mirth and closed the door behind them. "Let's get him up to bed."

Stony took his arm from around Demone. "I can make it there under my own steam."

"Cryin' out loud, Stony. There's no call to get so embarrassed." Although, he was looking kind of pale and that worried her.

"Who the hell said I'm embarrassed? I'm madder than spit at myself for not getting out of that son of Satan's way."

"Of course you are." She turned quickly, pressed her hand to her chest, took a deep breath. There. Sober as a judge. Not a dimple in sight. She had no idea what made her want to laugh, when this was a grave situation and her poor husband must be in awful pain. Was she getting hysterical? Had two panics in two days sent her around the bend?

"You go on up. I'll wait and let Chance in." She imagined Stony would appreciate the privacy. A big guy with a very delicate problem. And she didn't think a Snoopy bandage would work. A kiss might, but...

WHEN CHANCE CAME DOWNSTAIRS after seeing to Stony, he stopped in the kitchen.

"How is he?"

"Surly as a bear with a sore—well, you get it.

Nothing broken or bleeding. Just bruised. He'll be out of commission for a bit."

"Of course." Always the correct hostess, she took a mug off the shelf, when what she really wanted to do was run up the stairs and check on him for herself. "Would you like a cup of hot cider?"

"No. Grace shifted a couple of patients for me when Demone called. I'd better get back." He put a comforting hand on Eden's shoulder, his professional gaze moving over her skin tone, her eyes. "How about you? Any changes I should know about?"

Eden shrugged. "Um, I was late last month, then just had some spotting. No gully washers like before. I'm a little late right now. But both pregnancy tests have registered negative."

"You should come into the office, let me check you over, do some blood work."

She nodded. "I know. After the holidays, okay?" She wanted to at least make it through Christmas before she put herself back under the care of a professional who'd likely urge her to see the surgeon.

Right now, if she had to choose between the grim reaper and the knife, she'd choose the knife. She wanted to live. For Stony and Nikki. *With* Stony and Nikki.

She let Chance out and took a cup of hot cider up to the bedroom. Stony was sitting on the side of the bed wearing only his white briefs. A fire blazed in the fireplace, keeping the room nice and warm.

"What are you doing?" She put the cup on the nightstand and pulled back the covers. "You should be in bed."

He shook his head, looked up at her. "I want you to go."

"I told you before, there's no reason to be embarrassed."

"That's not what I'm talking about, Eden." Stony was aching, both below the belt and in his heart. This was the hardest thing he'd ever had to do. But their six months were almost up. "I can't make love to you."

"I know that." She smiled. "Honestly, did you think I was going to jump your bones?"

He didn't smile. He wanted to yell. He was always the one in control, the one who took care of everybody and everything. He didn't like giving up that control.

"This is your critical time, Eden. You've got to go. Find someone who can…" God, he hated to say it. "You've got to find somebody who can get you pregnant."

Her brows lowered along with her jaw. "Come again?"

"Don't make this any more difficult than it is. I know what having a baby means to you. I'd give anything in my power to make that happen for you, but I can't. I haven't. And now I'm practically useless."

She stared at him for a full five seconds. "Our six months aren't up yet." Her tone was chillingly polite, as though she was about to throw a shoe, but was too well-bred to do so.

He raked a hand through his hair. "I'm releasing you from that, Eden. Time's running out. You have to try for your dream."

She continued to stare at him, and for once he

had no idea what she was thinking, feeling. Her body was absolutely motionless; not rigid, but not relaxed, either. He began to sweat, feeling like a big idiot, sitting here in his underwear, admitting that he couldn't even get his own wife pregnant.

"I know what you're doing," she said, and simply spun on her booted heal and walked out of the room.

Stony's heart sank to his toes. How would he ever get along without her? How would he keep his sanity while she packed up her things? Walked out of his life? She'd accumulated a lot more stuff in the past six months. How was she going to fit it all in her little convertible?

And damn it, the roads were still too slippery for her to be zipping around in that sports car, regardless of the snow tires he'd put on it.

He heard the front door slam and frowned. Jaw clamped, wincing, he pushed himself off the bed and slowly moved to the hall. He called her name, didn't get an answer and felt his heart begin to knock violently beneath his ribs.

Limping, he made it over to the window just in time to see his truck shoot out of the driveway, the back end fishtailing like a sidewinder. He swore. She was going to get herself killed. Damn it, she was upset—he should have seen it—way too upset to be driving on slushy roads.

By God, he'd have to go after her. But where? He managed to get his jeans up, sucked in his breath when he worked the zipper, then pulled a sweatshirt over his head and tugged on socks and boots. Each step of the staircase had him swearing, sweating. In the kitchen he grabbed his coat off the rack and jammed his hat on his head. As he went to slam out the back door, a yellow sticky note stuck at eye level stopped him:

> Stony, if you're reading this, you ought to be ashamed, because the doctor told you to stay in bed. Nikki and I are at the Malones'—if you'll recall we were due for dinner. However, I'd appreciate it if you'd just stay home. I'm not in the mood to deal with you just yet.
>
>   Love, Eden.

"Not in the mood to deal with me?" Stony clamped his jaw and tugged the brim of his hat. "Guess we'll see about that."

EDEN MANAGED to get the truck stopped in front of the Malones' without taking out the porch. She was so upset she was actually shaking.

She lifted Nikki out of the truck, knocked on the back door, then walked on in. Distracted, she frowned when she saw her mother cooing over Hannah's baby and her father at the sink peeling potatoes.

"What are you two doing here?" she asked.

"We were invited, remember?" her mother said. "Dinner, then we're all going to town for the tree lighting."

No, she hadn't remembered. She looked around, trying to clear her mind, recall what was on the menu. Ah, the standing rib roast.

She glanced at Hannah, then Wyatt. "Do y'all need a cook? I'm hiring myself out. And if you don't mind, Nikki and I'd like to stay a spell."

Without waiting for an answer, and with her parents, the Callahans, the Malones, the old fellas and their wives staring at her oddly, she took off her gloves, hat and coat and went directly to the sink. Nobody in the room thought to challenge her.

"Daddy, sit down. I need to do this." She kissed his cheek, and he immediately relinquished his hold on the potato peeler and sat down. A smart man, he'd lived enough years in a houseful of women to know when to concede.

"I can't believe him," Eden ranted to no one in particular. "I told the damn man I loved him. A baby never even crossed my mind when he got injured." Violently, she set peeler to vegetable, taking half the potato with the peel.

"Darling," Sam objected. The judge laid a hand on her husband's shoulder, shook her head. With a sigh he sat back and tried not to cringe. "Well, really that's unnecessary."

The judge nodded, patted his hand. "I know, dear."

"Can you even *imagine* how he could even *think* that?" Eden asked. "Does he think I'm that horrible, that I'd be selfishly considering myself when he's hurt?"

"Um," Ethan ventured. "What injury would that be, Tex?"

She came out of her peeling frenzy, looked around the room. "I didn't tell you? Some stinkin' horse—devil horse is what Demone called it— kicked him right where it counts, if you know what I mean." The men crossed their legs. Eden ignored them. "I swear I wanted to hit him, regardless of the pain he was already in." She rinsed the potato and started massacring another. "And I know, Mama, that it's not ladylike or right to settle differences physically, but I was sorely tempted."

"Well," the judge said, "I suppose there are mitigating circumstances in any case." She lowered her voice, looked at the other occupants of the room. "Although, I'm just a bit lost at the moment. Happens a lot on the bench. I imagine we'll get it all sorted out sooner or later."

"Do you know what he suggested?" Eden pointed a knife she'd just picked up, slinging water on the floor. Sam lifted a hand, decided it would be fruitless to interrupt, and his wife quietly told him he was a wise man.

"He told me to go out and find somebody else to get me pregnant."

Now Beverley wanted to object. After all, there was a decent-size crowd in the kitchen, mixed company, and such a delicate subject. Sam patted her hand. He could be the calm one, since Eden had put down the knife. The carrots were in grave danger, but what was a carrot or two when their daughter was having a crisis. And such an interesting one at that.

"Like how?" Eden ranted. "Hang a sign around my neck and walk the highway? I am so mad I could just spit. That horse kicked him in the privates, but I think it affected his head—" Her tirade halted in midsentence at the sound of a very familiar masculine voice...swearing.

Uh-oh. Standing in the doorway was six feet five inches of bad attitude.

Utter silence engulfed the kitchen. Not a soul moved for several endless seconds.

Then Eden remembered she was just as mad—madder. "Cryin' out loud."

Stony advanced a step, stopped, fists clenched.

"Uh, sorry to hear about your…you know," Wyatt said.

"Nasty business," Ethan added, grinning.

Stony ignored them both. He was embarrassed that Eden had told the whole roomful of people the nature of his injury, but a haze of annoyance, worry and agony blocked out everything except the maddening woman standing across from him glaring back.

"What the hell possessed you to go tearing off like a maniac—on icy roads?"

"I did not tear off like a maniac." She drew her Southern dignity around her like a cloak.

"Of course not. My four-by-four just fishtailed all over the driveway for the hell of it. Woman, the way you constantly end up with one of the bumpers pointing in the wrong direction, you shouldn't even be allowed on the road."

She slammed the knife down on the counter. "*I* shouldn't be allowed on the road? *You* shouldn't be allowed out of bed. I think that horse scrambled your brains instead of your…" Her hand fluttered in the direction of his belt buckle. "And you *told* me to go."

He clenched his jaw so hard it was a wonder his back teeth didn't shatter. "I didn't mean that very minute." With a roomful of people looking on, he tried to explain himself once more, even though it was ripping him apart.

"Eden, it took a lot of courage and fierce want for you to ask a total stranger to get you pregnant and then marry him. I've seen the way you look at the babies, and it breaks my heart. And I've seen you nearly bleed to death before my eyes, seen the determination it takes to keep yourself on your feet, to fight your way through another month. That's why I told you to go.'' He dragged in a breath that literally hurt, tried to keep his voice even, quiet.

''Look, baby, we've tried for six months, and I've failed you. I don't expect you to stay. You'll be leaving, anyway, to go back to your business. I'm just urging you to go sooner. There's still time.''

Eden wiped her hands on her apron. She wanted to whack him. He'd called her ''baby'' in that tone that turned her to mush, but regardless the man was an idiot. Before she even realized her intentions, she'd grabbed a sugar cookie off a plate and hurled it at him, beaning him square on the jaw.

He didn't react, didn't so much as blink.

Eden was appalled at what she'd actually done, and she held her breath, as did everyone else in the room.

She ought to apologize. Instead she said, ''It's just what you deserve. You're talking nonsense and—''

''I love you, damn it! And because of that I'm willing to sacrifice,'' he shouted. ''I can let you go so you can get your baby. Why the *hell* are you being so stubborn!''

Eden was so stunned by Stony's outburst she nearly sat down. When her Mustang had slid backward into the barn, he'd been livid, but he hadn't shouted. He wasn't a man to raise his voice. That's what made him such a good horse trainer. His even temper, his gentleness and deep voice.

Well, up jumped the devil, she thought, and noticed that hers wasn't the only jaw hanging open.

He shut his eyes. "Eden…"

That single word, just the one, was filled with so much agony and so much love, Eden felt as though she'd been handed the moon and the stars, as well.

She stepped up to him, placed her hand over his heart, rubbed. "Why am I being so stubborn?" she repeated softly. "Because I love you more. More than having a baby. More than a house in Texas, more than Garden of Eden—I sold it, by the way."

"You…?"

She nodded, noticed his hand had covered hers, didn't imagine he even realized it. "I don't need to get pregnant, Stony. If it doesn't happen, it just doesn't. But I *do* need you and Nikki. I have all the family I could ever want right here." She deliberately placed her hand over his scar, stroked, leaned into him and pressed her lips to the side of his eye. "I love being your wife," she whispered. "I love your strength, the way you make me feel. I love exactly who you are. I don't want six months, I want a lifetime."

His Adam's apple bobbed several times as he swallowed. He searched her face, his gaze like a caress. Then he took her face between his big palms, tipped up her chin and lightly, reverently pressed his lips to hers.

"I'm rescinding my sacrificial offer. I love you, Eden. You are my heart," he rasped. "I won't ever let you go now."

"Well, I hope to shout."

His lips curved, slowly, fully, and his eyes went

hot. Eden's heart pounded. Lord have mercy, she knew that look.

Holding her gaze, he took her wrists, locked them around his neck, then slid his palms down the sides of his arms, all the way down her waist. He bent his knees, pulled her tight against him and stood. Eden knew she was going to spend a good portion of the rest of her life with her feet off the floor. When she felt his arousal pressed against her, her eyes widened. She'd forgotten…

"Stony, your—"

"Hurts like a son of a gun, but obviously works just fine."

"Still, maybe we shouldn't—"

"I'm going to kiss you now, wild thing. You might want to pay attention."

"There are people—oh!" Holding her with one arm, he slid his hand to the back of her neck, angled her head and kissed the living daylights out of her. Oh, yes, she was definitely paying attention. His lips were gentle, yet aggressive, assertive….

He eased up, never broke contact, said against her lips. "I love you, baby. I'll try to be all that you need." Before she could tell him he *was* all that she needed, he drew her right back into the kiss, seducing her, turning her mindless, boneless and so in love she thought she'd burst. He kissed her long after it was polite or proper, without apology, without a care for the dozen or so people looking on.

When he finally lifted his head, Eden couldn't even remember what day it was, didn't think she could speak or breathe. "Cryin' out loud."

Stony's laughter boomed out, and he twirled her around. "I am so crazy about you."

Everyone in the room who knew Stony—knew that he rarely laughed so unrestrained—gaped for an astonished second, then smiled, mouths stretched wide, hearts rejoicing.

The judge broke the spell when she leaned forward and crooked a finger at Nikki. "Here, doll, come let Grandma see what you've got."

Nikki looked so hopeful, Eden felt tears sting.

"Well, your daddy's married to my little girl, that makes you your grandmother." Beverley's alto voice was even toned and completely unruffled—the voice of a judge. She accepted the tiny sticks Nikki and Ian had been playing with.

"We was just havin' a sword fight. I winned and Rosie says the winner gets to keep both swords."

"Rosie is quite the smart dog." Even though she was several miles away on an entirely different ranch. "Let's see what we have here." She held up one stick. "A single pink line." She lifted the other. "Two pink lines. I'd hazard a guess that these wonderful children have introduced into evidence the results of a pregnancy test—one negative, the other positive."

Beverley's gaze rested softly on Eden, then back down to Nikki. "And they make fine swords, doll, but tell us all how you came by them."

"I took 'em out of the trash. I showed Ian at Thanksgiving, but Dora fell out—that means fainting case you didn't know—and we couldn't play. And then Rosie wanted the glass and it breaked all over the floor. I had to get the snoopy bandage and I liked *that* one in the trash 'cuz it had *two* pink lines like my candy cane."

"And you switched them," Beverley coached.

"Yep. But Rosie wanted to play, too, and she told me to go get the other one, 'cuz it was in the trash anyway and nobody wanted it."

Beverley lifted Nikki into her lap and hugged her. "And Grandma's very proud that you're such a wonderful friend to share with Rosie and Ian this way." She looked up, the picture of calm, as though she'd sifted through all the evidence and was at last able to render her judgment.

Holding up the two sticks, she asked, "Eden, darlin' do you recognize these items as yours?"

Eden nodded. Her lips were numb.

"And could you enlighten us as to which one says there's a baby?"

Eden, standing on her feet now, had to grab Stony's arm for balance. Blood shot to her head, and her heart pounded. "Two lines," she whispered.

Nikki's eyes widened, and she craned her neck to have another look at the strips. "Where's the baby?" she demanded, as though someone had hidden it. Then she looked at Eden. "Is the baby in your tummy?"

Eden looked up at Stony. "I think so."

"Okay. I want a sister. But Daddy shouldn't yell anymore 'cuz it scared me half to death." Everyone laughed because Nikki was always so secure and matter-of-fact. "And can you really and truly be my mommy now? 'Cuz Daddy loves you to bits, and he loves me to bits, too, and Rosie said the baby wants me to call you Mommy 'cuz you are, 'cuz you give me kisses and Snoopy bandages and call me sugar and make cookies with the M&M faces and let Rosie help lick the beaters."

Eden was really afraid she was going to start

bawling and embarrass herself. Her heart was so full she didn't know what to do with all the emotion. "I think Rosie is very smart, and I want to be your mommy more than anything."

"Okay." Nikki hopped down off Beverley's lap, raced over to Eden and handed her the pregnancy sticks. "Here's the baby. Let's go play, Ian."

Stony cupped Eden's hand, raised it, looked at the two strips, then leaned down and touched her lips with his. She thought she'd experienced every facet of Stony Stratton's tenderness. In that single, heartfelt brush of his lips, she learned that her husband was and always would be full of wonderful surprises.

And she was the lucky woman who got to be his wife.

AND WHILE EDEN AND STONY melted every single heart in the room, Ozzie Peyton unashamedly wiped a white handkerchief over his vivid-blue eyes. Lloyd, Vern and Henry all slapped him on the back, each of them taking credit for the happy ending.

"Yes, sir, the next baby of Shotgun Ridge'll be born late next summer. Gonna have us a regular baby boom, you bet."

All because of their matchmaking skills, Ozzie thought, raising his eyes heavenward. He'd like to think that his Vanessa was watching and smiling down on them.

Stony and Eden would make a fine family together, you bet. And it was all because of him and the boys.

They were getting pretty darn good at laying the path and getting these recalcitrant cowboys to walk on down it. Ought to make a business out of it, you bet. A nudging service…

***Don't miss
an exciting opportunity
to save on the purchase of
Harlequin and Silhouette books!***

Buy any two Harlequin or
Silhouette books and save
$10.00 off future Harlequin
and Silhouette purchases

OR

buy any three
Harlequin or Silhouette books
and save **$20.00 off** future
Harlequin and Silhouette purchases.

***Watch for details
coming in October 2000!***

PHQ400

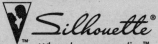

Daddy's little girl... **THAT'S MY BABY!** by

Vicki Lewis Thompson

Nat Grady is finally home—older and wiser. When the woman he'd loved had hinted at commitment, Nat had run far and fast. But now he knows he can't live without her. But Jessica's nowhere to be found.

Jessica Franklin is living a nightmare. She'd thought things were rough when the man she loved ran out on her, leaving her to give birth to their child alone. But when she realizes she has a stalker on her trail, she has to run—and the only man who can help her is Nat Grady.

THAT'S MY BABY!

On sale September 2000 at your favorite retail outlet.

HARLEQUIN®
Makes any time special ™